OUTWIT · OUTPLAY

SURVIVOR

OUTLAST

™

THAILAND
by Erica Pass

SIMON SPOTLIGHT
NEW YORK   LONDON   TORONTO   SYDNEY

This book is a work of fiction. Any references to historical events, real people, or real locales are used fictitiously. Other names, characters, places, and incidents are the product of the author's imagination, and any resemblance to actual events or locales or persons, living or dead, is entirely coincidental.

Based on the TV series *Survivor* created by Mark Burnett as seen on CBS

SIMON SPOTLIGHT
An imprint of Simon & Schuster Children's Publishing Division
1230 Avenue of the Americas, New York, New York 10020
© 2005 Survivor Productions, LLC. All rights reserved. The SURVIVOR LOGO is a trademark of Survivor Productions, LLC. Used under license from CBS Consumer Products, CBS Enterprises, a Division of CBS Broadcasting Inc.

SIMON SPOTLIGHT and colophon are registered trademarks of Simon & Schuster, Inc.

Manufactured in the United States of America

First Edition
10 9 8 7 6 5 4 3 2 1

ISBN 0-689-87708-0

Library of Congress Catalog Card Number 2004112376

It was sunrise when the ten competitors arrived via boat at Koh Tarutao, an island off the coast of Thailand. Some looked calm. Others looked excited. All were nervous. They knew that their lives were about to change. But were they ready for it?

The ten sat on the sand, looking around at one another. A young man approached, striding toward them as he carried some objects with both arms. He was tall, with dark hair and eyes, and wore khaki shorts with a crisp white T-shirt and brown leather sandals. When he reached them, he freed his arms of what turned out to be ten folded chairs, each with a stretch of blue canvas attached to metal legs.

"I'm Jake," he said. "Come on up and take a chair."

The players each came up to secure a chair and then returned to their original spots in the sand.

"Welcome," he said after everyone was settled. "You're now on Koh Tarutao, which will be your new home for however long you last in the game. You're all here because you have different strengths and interests. Now, whether or not you have what it takes to be the ultimate Survivor—that's another story.

"You're all from different parts of the United States, but I can assure you that none of you has ever had an experience quite like *Survivor*. We purposely planned this game so monsoon season is long over, but you'll still have plenty of challenges. Finding adequate food and water. Creating shelter. And just adapting to a new habitat, with animals and insects that you're not used to. Last but not least, you'll need to learn how to work with your teammates, who may become friends, but who will also be competitors. And let's not forget—you're all after the same prize—two hundred *thousand* dollars.

"Yes, this will be the experience of a lifetime. But it's not going to be easy! You guys will be competing in a series of challenges throughout the time you're here. Some will be Reward Challenges, in which you'll be playing for prizes, and some will be Immunity Challenges, in which the winner is granted Immunity from an upcoming Tribal Council."

He paused and held up a picture of an elephant.

"Two of you will find an elephant just like this one marked underneath the seat of your chair. Elephants have a long, rich history in Thailand; they are revered creatures. Go ahead, check."

Jake waited as the ten looked beneath their chairs.

"Got it!" a petite girl called out right before the deeper voice of a tall boy yelled out, "Me too!"

"Great," said Jake. "You two, come up by me. What are your names?"

"Lily," said the girl as she brushed off some sand from her knees.

"Peter," said the boy. They both shook Jake's hand.

"Okay, Lily and Peter," said Jake. "Here's the scoop. I want each of you to pick the next member of your team. But you need to pick someone of the opposite sex."

Lily and Peter both chose. The second member of each team was then given the same instruction: pick someone of the opposite sex. This went on until each team had five members.

"Okay," said Jake. We're going to need team names for you guys. We'll give you a list of words—in both Thai and English—and you'll need to agree on one that you think symbolizes your team. That's your first assignment."

The two groups headed off to separate tables that had been set up by the water. There were platters of fresh mango waiting for them.

To hear about Peter's group, turn to page 6.
To hear about Lily's group, turn to page 9.

The five sat around the table glancing at one another. A small boy with an olive complexion and green eyes introduced himself as Carlos and then started eating the mango. And eating some more . . .

"Hey," Peter said. "Save some for the rest of us."

"Oh, come on," said a girl with freckles and curly auburn hair held back by a bandanna. "He's just hungry." She looked around at the rest of the group. "How about we get to know each other?"

Another girl, around thirteen, smiled. "I second that. Why don't we tell each other a little bit about ourselves?"

"There's a game I know that could help," said the first girl. "Why don't we each come up with a word to describe ourselves . . . with the catch being that the word has to start with the same letter as our first name?"

The group nodded, including Carlos, who had stopped snatching mango as soon as Peter had snapped at him.

"Sounds babyish, but whatever," said Peter. He smoothed a hand over his blond hair and put on a baseball cap. "Why don't you start, bandanna girl?"

"Okay," she answered, glaring at him. "I will. I'm Hannah. I'm from Philadelphia. And you guys can call me Harmonious Hannah."

"Because you like people to get along?" asked Peter.

"Well, yes," Hannah answered. "But also because I love music. I love singing it and I love writing it. Especially jazz."

"Cool," the other girl said. She was lean and athletic-looking, and her dark hair was in several braids secured with tiny beads that clanged when she shook her head. "I'll go next. My name is April. And my adjective is *adventurous*. I can't wait to try lots of new things here."

"And I'm Cross-country Carlos!" said Carlos. "'Cause I love to run. I'm on the cross-country team at my school. I may be little, but I'm fast."

"Powerful Peter," said Peter. "And I say we pick our team name already."

"Wait," said April. She turned to the final team member, a boy who had been using a stick as if it was a pencil, making doodles on the table. He had shaggy dark hair, wore glasses, and his shoulders were hunched over, making him appear smaller than he actually was. "What's your adjective? I mean, name?"

He looked up. "My name is Will . . . but I can't think of any adjectives. . . ."

"Hmmm," said Hannah. "Well, looks like you like to draw. . . ."

Will shrugged. "Yeah, but artistic doesn't start with a *W*."

"No," said April. "But whimsical does! Okay. So we have Powerful Peter. Cross-country Carlos. Harmonious Hannah. Whimsical Will. And me, Adventurous April. Cool. Now let's pick our team name."

The five teammates looked down at the list of words in front of them.

"Hey," said Carlos. "How about *courage*? We're going to need lots of that, right?"

"Courage," said Peter. "I like it."

"Me too," said Hannah. "What's the translation?"

"Courage is . . . *kwam gla,*" said April. "Will, what do you think? Kwam Gla cool with you?"

Will smiled at April and nodded.

"Should we vote?" April asked. She lifted her hand. "All those in favor of Kwam Gla, raise your hands." She looked around at five raised hands and cheered. "Kwam Gla it is!"

To hear about Lily's group, turn to page 9.
To move on to the first Reward Challenge, turn to page 11.

The five new teammates glanced at one another without saying a word, occasionally picking up pieces of mango. Finally Lily, a petite girl with a cocoa-colored complexion and wide brown eyes, climbed on top of the table, where she sat cross-legged.

"Since no one else has volunteered, I'll go first," she said, tucking some of her black hair behind one ear. "I'm Lily, and I'm from Hawaii, so I know a little something about island living. I'm twelve and I love yoga and dance." She looked at the boy to her right, who was lanky and wore long shorts that were frayed at the edges. He had what looked like a homemade bracelet made of thread on his left wrist. "What's your name?"

"I'm Randy. I'm also twelve. And I love the outdoors, but I know nothing about living on an island, so I'll be grateful for the advice. I'm from Colorado."

"Is there anything else we should know about you?" asked Lily.

"Well, I like magic," said Randy. "So watch out, or I might make some of you disappear." He wiggled his fingers out in front of his body as if he was casting a spell.

"Heh," laughed a girl next to him who was wearing a Yankees baseball cap. "That's not magic, that's playing the game! I'm Zoe. I'm thirteen and from New York City. I love to kickbox—and eat pizza."

"I don't think you'll find too much pizza here," said a tall girl next to her with long blond hair and freckles. "My name's Brenna. I grew up on a farm. . . . I miss my family a lot. And my horses. But I think this is going to be fun. Oh, and I'm fourteen."

"Well, that leaves me," said a boy sitting at the head of the table. He was the least athletic-looking one in the group, and wore pants and a button-down shirt. His hair was shaved very close to his scalp, and he wore wire-rimmed glasses. "I'm Samuel. I'm thirteen. And I love politics, so I can't wait to start strategizing," Samuel said, rubbing his hands together.

The others looked around a little nervously. Except for Zoe. She rarely looked nervous, even when she was.

Lily placed the list of Thai words on the table. "So . . . we need to choose a name for our team." They all looked at the list together.

"*Adventure*?" asked Zoe.

"*Strength*?" suggested Samuel.

"How about *destiny*?" said Brenna. "Look, *Pom likit* means 'destiny.'"

"Destiny," said Lily. "I like it!"

"I guess that's what it's all about, right?" said Randy.

"Show of hands?" said Samuel. Five hands went up. "Pom Likit it is!"

To continue, turn to page 11.

"Great," said Jake as both teams returned to him with their selections. "Congratulations, Pom Likit and Kwam Gla. Now, are you ready for your first Reward Challenge?"

Everyone nodded.

"What are we playing for?" asked Peter.

Jake gestured behind him, where there were five wicker baskets neatly stacked. "The winning team will be given these baskets, which are ideal for gathering food," he said. "In addition, that team will be given a map of the island detailing all the best food-gathering sites."

He led both teams over to a wall constructed of bamboo. "Welcome," he said, "to *Bamboo*zled. We've constructed two identical mazes completely out of bamboo. Each team has to find its way through the maze by depending on and trusting one another. The catch is that each team also needs to form a human chain. Each of you must be touching another member of your team at all times. We'll send someone along with each team to make sure this is done. If at any point the chain is broken, your team will be sent back to the starting line. First team to make it out of the maze wins." He looked around as the kids arranged themselves by the two mazes. "Ready? On your mark . . . get set . . . GO!"

If you want Kwam Gla to win the Reward Challenge, turn to page 12.
If you want Pom Likit to win the Reward Challenge, turn to page 14.

From the start April kept spirits high as she led the way through the maze, the five players holding hands.

"Wait!" yelled Carlos at a fork in the maze. He started tugging on April's hand, almost causing her to lose her grip.

"Carlos," she said, exasperated. "Cut it out. You're going to lose the entire challenge for us."

Carlos sulked but allowed April to lead him back.

"Don't wreck this for the rest of us," said Peter, sneering at Carlos.

"I get it!" shouted Carlos. "I won't do it again."

"Look," said Hannah, using her chin to gesture to the right. "I think I see the beach up ahead."

Indeed she was right, and the team carefully made their way to the finish line, beating Pom Likit, who were also fighting over in their bamboo maze.

"This way," said Zoe, tilting her head to the right. She held Brenna's hand in her right hand and Randy's in her left.

"No," said Samuel, "you're totally wrong. That way," he said, using his nose to point to the left.

"You guys," said Brenna. "We can't stand here all day."

Just then they heard cheering from Kwam Gla, and Jake found them in the maze. He rapped his knuckles on the bamboo wall.

"Come on," he said. "Your time's up."

Back on the beach, Pom Likit watched dejectedly as Kwam Gla received their baskets and map.

"Next time," Samuel said to his teammates, "we

can't waste so much time." He looked directly at Zoe.

Meanwhile Kwam Gla raced around the island, discovering hidden places for fruit and shellfish that they never would have known about without the map. Carlos shimmied up trees to collect coconuts, which he tossed down to April, who placed them in her basket. Will collected some leaves which, according to the map, were edible. And Hannah and Peter went down to the water to search for clams and crabs. One thing was for sure: they wouldn't be going hungry during their time on Koh Tarutao.

To continue, turn to page 16.

"We need to stick together," said Lily, grasping one of Zoe's hands and one of Samuel's. "Whatever you do, don't let go."

"I say we go that way," said Samuel, nodding his head to the right.

"No," said Randy. "Let's go left. There are more twists to the left; I think the right is a dead end."

"Let's vote on it," said Samuel. "Without raising any hands, who wants to go right, besides me?"

It was silent.

"Fine," Samuel said. "I can go along with majority rule. We'll go left. But if I'm right, don't expect me not to say 'I told you so.'"

"I bet you're really good at that," said Zoe, smirking.

Luckily for Pom Likit, Randy's hunch was correct, and they ended up making it out of the maze a few minutes later.

Kwam Gla, on the other hand, had their hands full with Carlos, who kept pulling ahead.

"Carlos," yelled Peter. "Chill!"

"But I have a good feeling about this," said Carlos excitedly. He yanked on Hannah's hand, and at the same time tripped on a mound of dirt, sending both him and Hannah flying. They lost their grip and the chain was broken.

The adult escort helped them up and led them back to the start, but by that time, Pom Likit had already won.

"You're gonna pay for that," Peter said to Carlos.

Back at the meeting place Jake handed out the baskets to the members of Pom Likit.

"This is awesome!" said Zoe. "Now I think I can learn to live without pizza for a while." The team slapped hands as Kwam Gla looked on.

"Don't worry, guys," said April. "We'll rally in the next challenge." But even she looked a little doubtful as Pom Likit raced by, eager to use their prize.

To continue, turn to page 16.

After the challenge the tribes returned to their respective campsites. Back at Kwam Gla, Peter was taking a nap as April and Hannah prepared dinner.

"He naps a lot," said Hannah.

"I noticed," said April.

"And when he's not napping," Hannah continued, "he doesn't shut up."

"I noticed that, too," said April. She continued shelling shrimp, leaving the translucent coverings in a pile at her feet.

"Just something to keep an eye on," said Hannah, quieting down as Carlos and Will returned from the woods, where they had gathered more coconuts. They sat down to crack them open and get at the milk. The four worked for another half an hour to prepare the meal.

Peter awoke just in time to eat.

Meanwhile all five members of Pom Likit were hard at work. Randy was thatching together mats out of bamboo for them to sleep on while Zoe, Lily, and Brenna prepared oysters and clams for dinner. Samuel was making trips back and forth to the nearby water source, collecting buckets of water that they would later have to boil before drinking in order to sterilize it.

"How do you guys feel so far?" asked Zoe.

"Okay," said Lily carefully.

"Fine," said Brenna.

"Oh, stop being so polite," said Zoe. "You can be real with me. I'm not sure how I feel about Samuel. I thought maybe the three of us could think about forming an alliance, in case we don't win Immunity."

"Why wouldn't we win Immunity?" said Lily.

"Zoe's right," said Brenna. "We need to start thinking about strategy. After all, Sam is."

"Right," said Zoe. "And I don't want to get caught without a plan. So, are you in?"

"Let's give it a day or two," said Lily. "Then we'll talk."

"I'll think about it," said Brenna.

"Fine," said Zoe. "But be careful. He's probably already planned out exactly how he's gonna win this whole thing."

To continue, turn to page 18.

After two days of getting to know one another and getting acclimated to Koh Tarutao, it was time for the first Immunity Challenge. The teams gathered on the beach, and Jake called for their attention.

"Your next challenge," he said, "will be for the Immunity idol." He held up a small primitive-looking figure made out of clay. "This idol will protect your team from going to Tribal Council. You all know that the Tribal Council is an integral part of the game. It's where a team must vote one of its own off the island.

"Today's challenge is a game we like to call 'Tic-Tac-Oh-No!' It's just like regular tic-tac-toe, with one exception. You guys will be human Xs and Os . . . or in this case, Ps, for Pom Likit, and Ks, for Kwam Gla."

Jake handed out some signs that had been marked with Ps and Ks for the competitors to wear around their necks during the game.

"Each team will need to nominate a leader to call the shots. But keep in mind that as long as you're not actually on the board yet, you can discuss your next move as a team."

The two teams huddled and then announced that Samuel would be the leader for Pom Likit and Hannah would be the leader for Kwam Gla.

If you want Tic-Tac-Oh-No! to be played on land, turn to page 19.
If you want Tic-Tac-Oh-No!" to be played in the water, turn to page 20.

After a coin toss, it was determined that Kwam Gla would go first. Hannah sent April to the top right square, while Samuel placed Randy in the center. One by one they went, until all the teammates except the leaders had gone in. No one had won.

"We need to call it a draw and try again," said Brenna.

Both teams hopped off the board and got ready to play another round. Again, a draw. And another.

They played for over half an hour with the same results. Finally Samuel began to notice a similar pattern emerging from Kwam Gla and took advantage of that by predicting their moves.

"Lily, take center square," Samuel advised. Hannah placed Carlos next to her.

"Randy," said Samuel. "Upper right corner."

Hannah was tiring. She placed April in the slot above Carlos, unfortunately not seeing that Samuel would then have an opportunity to win for Pom Likit.

"Brenna," Samuel said calmly. "Lower left corner."

Hannah smacked her hand to her forehead as she realized her mistake.

"Pom Likit," announced Jake. "This time around, Immunity is yours."

To return to Kwam Gla's camp before Tribal Council, turn to page 21.
To go straight to the first Tribal Council, turn to page 22.

"There's just one more thing before we start," said Jake. "You'll be playing out there." He pointed to the water, where nine wooden posts were set up in a grid formation. There was a small platform at the top of each post.

"It's going to involve a lot of balancing," Jake added. "If you fall off, your team will immediately be disqualified."

Pom Likit won the coin toss and started first.

"Zoe," said Samuel, "go out to center square." Zoe hesitated. She told her team that she wasn't a strong swimmer. She dog-paddled her way slowly out to the post and climbed up, relieved to be out of the water.

Hannah sent Will out, who took his place next to Zoe. Samuel then sent Lily to a post on the other side of Zoe.

"It's slippery up here!" said Lily as Hannah sent Carlos swimming toward her.

"Careful!" said Carlos, taunting Lily as he climbed up his post. "Wouldn't want to fall off, now would you?"

Except Lily hadn't been exaggerating. Almost as soon as Carlos stood up, he wobbled and fell off the post, banging his elbow as he slid into the water.

"Don't worry. I *won't* say I told you so," said Lily.

Carlos grumbled in the water, rubbing his elbow. Will swam over to him to see if he was okay. Hannah, Peter, and April watched from the shore, shaking their heads as the members of Pom Likit cheered.

To return to Kwam Gla's camp before Tribal Council, turn to page 21.
To go straight to Tribal Council, turn to page 22.

Things were quiet as the team prepared for the first Tribal Council. Hannah had talked to Peter about helping out more, and he was now chopping some wood so they could build a container to store food. Hannah and April watched from a distance.

"So," said Hannah. "I'm thinking about voting for Peter."

"Yeah," said April. "You don't like him very much. But he's pretty strong. I think he might be good to keep around and help us win competitions."

"He might just drive me crazy," said Hannah.

April shrugged. "I want our team to win as many challenges as we can. And as nice as Will is, I don't think he's our best bet for winning."

Meanwhile Carlos approached Peter to help him break apart the wood.

"Peter," said Carlos. "Who are you voting for?"

"First you tell me who *you're* voting for," said Peter.

"Well," said Carlos. "I'm not sure. I was hoping you could give me some advice."

"Will," said Peter. "He's weak. He doesn't belong here."

Carlos nodded. "Okay," he said. "Will it is." He continued chopping wood alongside Peter. Peter grinned, slowly realizing how handy it would be to have Carlos do whatever he said.

To continue, turn to page 22.

That evening the five members of Kwam Gla headed to Tribal Council uneasily.

"Come on, guys," said April. "Look on the bright side. The person who goes home doesn't have to eat mango ever again!"

"I *like* mango," said Carlos.

"How is everyone?" asked Jake as the five took their seats.

"Nervous," said Hannah. "I'm not ready to go home."

"Do you think you have any reason to worry about that at this point?" asked Jake.

Hannah shrugged. "You never know."

"I'm going to give each of you a slip of paper," said Jake. "One at a time, you'll approach the urn, where you will find a pen to write your vote with. When you've done that, place the piece of paper in the urn and return to your seat. All voting is confidential, and majority vote rules. I'll tally the votes in front of you."

The five cast their votes, and Jake went to retrieve the urn. One by one he unfurled the slips of paper, holding each one up as he did.

"One for Will," he said, "and one for Peter."

Peter glared around him, trying to figure out who had voted for him.

"Another one for Will . . . and another for Peter," continued Jake.

April, Hannah, and Carlos breathed a sigh of relief, knowing they were safe for this round. Peter's fists were clenched, while Will had his head leaning against one hand, his cheek against his palm.

Jake unwrapped the final piece of paper and looked up. "And one more for Will."

Will walked slowly up to Jake, holding his torch.

"Will, I'm sorry to see you go," Jake said as he snuffed out Will's torch. "But the tribe has spoken."

"That's okay," said Will. "I don't think I'm cut out for this kind of game anyway."

Slowly he turned and was immediately escorted off the tribal site.

"Everyone else," said Jake, "back to camp."

"That was really hard," said April as Kwam Gla returned to their makeshift camp.

Peter shrugged. "It's all in the name of the game."

"Yeah, well, building our shelter is *also* in the name of the game," said Hannah. "And we all need to chip in and help. At least Will was cooperative."

"What are you saying?" Peter asked. "I help plenty."

Hannah rolled her eyes.

"Come on, guys," said April. "Arguing isn't going to get our shelter built."

"I'm beat," said Peter. "Tomorrow morning we'll finish collecting the leaves and sticks we need."

Meanwhile the teammates of Pom Likit sat around their camp. They had been lucky to be assigned a home base that included the natural shelter of a cave. They were listening now as Brenna played her guitar.

"I wonder how Tribal Council is going," said Randy.

"That's the worst part of being here," said Lily. "I don't think so," said Samuel. "This is a *game*."

"I know," replied Lily. "But it just makes me sad to send people home. Especially the first one to go. . . . We've only been here a few days."

"Get used to it, Lily," said Samuel.

"He's right," said Zoe. "And it's only going to get harder."

To see what happened the next morning at Kwam Gla's camp, turn to page 25.
To see what happened the next morning at Pom Likit's camp, turn to page 26.
To go straight to the next Reward Challenge, turn to page 27.

The next morning everyone awoke to rain. It splashed in the faces of the Kwam Gla tribe as they lay curled on their bamboo mats.

"Nice alarm clock," muttered Peter.

"Great," said Hannah sarcastically. "*Now* how are we supposed to finish building our shelter?"

The team huddled under the part of their shelter that they'd completed, which barely protected them.

April stood up, tying a bandanna around her head. "I'll go."

Peter stared up at her. "What's your rush? Just wait it out."

April shook her head. "It's not that bad. And I want to get this done already."

Carlos jumped up. "I'll go with you."

"And I'll go collect some food," Hannah offered. "Everyone like crab?"

The three of them set off while Peter sat underneath the shelter. He lay down and was soon fast asleep and snoring.

To continue, turn to page 27.

When the tribe awoke the next morning, Brenna was missing.

Randy peered out from the cave. "Where could she have gone?" he said.

"She's been really sad lately," said Lily. "I think she really misses home."

Zoe joined them at the opening of the cave, hands on hips. "She'll be fine," she said. "Come on, we have to go find some food."

Lily stared at her. "You don't care about Brenna?"

"How far could she have gone?" asked Zoe.

"I'm sure she's fine, Lily," said Samuel, squinting out at the light rain.

"That's not the point," Lily said. "She's upset." She turned to Randy. "We can go look for food and Brenna at the same time."

"Good idea," Randy said. "We'll get some crabs and hopefully some oysters. Zoe, can you and Sam go gather berries and plants?"

"Wait a minute," said Zoe. "Plants? You can eat plants here?"

Lily rolled her eyes. "Randy, why don't you and Sam go down to the water. I'll take City Girl here to get some plants, since I know which ones are edible."

Lily and Zoe set off. "Just be careful of snakes," Lily said as they ambled away. "They like to hang out in tree branches."

"*What?!*" cried Zoe.

To continue, turn to page 27.

The next day both teams gathered at their central meeting place on the beach. Unlike yesterday, the sun was out in full force, beating down on their heads and drying up any remaining dampness.

"Greetings, Survivors," said Jake. "How are you all doing?"

"Better, now that we're dry," said Hannah. "We finished our shelter. Well, I should say, *most* of us finished our shelter." She looked directly at Peter.

"Whatever, Hannah," said Peter. "I helped boil those stupid crabs, which, by the way, are gross."

"As you can see," April said to Jake, "we're having a few issues."

"But overall," said Carlos, "it's still pretty cool to be here."

"Okay," said Jake. "Pom Likit? How are you guys faring?"

"How come you didn't tell us there are snakes here?" asked Zoe. "I hate snakes."

Jake laughed. "Just be cautious, and you'll be fine."

"I like the team, and our campsite is great," said Brenna. "But I miss home. A lot."

Lily put her arm around her.

"The cave rocks," said Randy. "It kept us dry yesterday."

"You guys have a cave?" asked Carlos. "That's so unfair!"

"They do," said Jake, "but your team is much closer to the water source. So don't complain.

"Well, let's get started. Your next Reward Challenge

is a little different. This challenge is called 'Sing a Song,' and you won't be racing through a maze or playing a game. You'll need to rely on other skills.

"There are two parts. First you'll get half an hour to come up with a song or cheer for your team. You'll need to work on the words together, and then one of you should record it, line by line. There will be pencils and paper at each of your meeting sites for you to use. When time is up, you'll need to hand in your written song."

"And then?" asked Zoe.

"And then," said Jake, "I'll tell you what to do next. One bit of advice. Pay attention to what you're writing down—once you give the paper to me, you won't be able to see it again. Okay. Begin."

To watch Kwam Gla work on their song, turn to page 29.
To watch Pom Likit work on their song, turn to page 30.

Right away April turned to Hannah. "You *own* this challenge! You're all about music!"

Hannah smiled. "I *do* have some ideas."

"I think I should rap," said Peter.

"Yeah, that would be cool," said Carlos.

"Do either of you know the first thing about rapping?" asked Hannah.

"Whatever," said Peter. "How hard could it be?"

"Pretty hard," said Hannah. Peter scowled, but he handed the pencil to her.

To continue, turn to page 31.

"Okay," Samuel said. "Here's what we should do."

"Last time I checked, this was a team, Sam," said Zoe. "We shouldn't *do* anything except work together."

"I think Brenna knows more about music than any of us," said Lily.

"Oh, I just play guitar," said Brenna quietly.

"Yeah," said Lily. "Well, that's more than me."

"Me too," said Randy. He handed the pencil to Brenna.

To continue, turn to page 31.

After thirty minutes the two teams returned to the original meeting place, where Jake was waiting for them.

"Okay," said Jake. "How'd you do?"

"Our cheer kicks butt," said Carlos.

"No way," Zoe shot back. "Ours rules!"

"I'm sure they're both fine," said Jake. "Think you guys know your stuff?"

Everyone nodded.

"Know it *well*?" asked Jake.

Again, nods all around.

"Great," said Jake. "Come on up and hand me what you've got. And go take a swim."

"A swim?" asked Brenna.

"Yup," said Jake. "The challenge isn't over—you're getting a break. It's hot. You deserve it. Meet back here in thirty minutes."

Everyone ran into the water.

After a long swim the groups reassembled.

"Feel good?" asked Jake. "Refreshed?"

The group nodded.

"Great," continued Jake. "I need you guys to line up. Pom Likit over here," he motioned to his right, "and Kwam Gla over here." He motioned to his left.

"Remember when I asked if you knew your cheers well?" he asked. "Well, I hope the swim didn't erase them from your memories. I'm going to ask you guys to recite your cheer. Each teammate should recite a line. First we'll do a coin toss. Heads, Kwam Gla goes first; tails, Pom Likit goes first."

Kwam Gla won the coin toss and looked expectantly to Jake for instructions.

"Do you guys want to go first or second?" he asked.

"Let's get it over with," said April.

"Okay," said Jake. "Line up and recite the cheer. One line per person. I have the words here, so I'll know if you're faking."

Hannah bit her lip and lined up next to her teammates. They all looked confident. "I'll start," she said, taking a deep breath.

"We are Kwam Gla," she began.

"Here to say," added Peter.

"We've got courage," from April.

"You'd best run away," said Carlos.

"Just because," from Hannah.

"We lost one friend," said Peter.

"Doesn't mean we won't," said April.

"Last till the end," said Carlos.

All four of them then chanted, "Go, fight, win! Kwam Gla!"

Hannah beamed. They'd done it!

Jake nodded. "Very nice. That was perfect, actually." He looked over at Pom Likit. "You guys have a tough act to follow. Kwam Gla has secured their prize. . . . If you can perform as well as they did, there just may be enough to go around."

Samuel turned and looked at his team and then hissed, "Don't mess up."

"Remember, the beginning is all of us," said Brenna as the team recited "Go, Pom Likit!" a few times.

"Brenna, Zoe, Lily, and Sam," said Randy.

"Add on Randy, he's our man," said Zoe.

"No need to run," said Brenna.

"No need to hide," said Lily.

"But know that we're winners . . . ," started Samuel. "Wait . . . just accept . . . um . . ."

Pom Likit stared at Samuel in disbelief.

"Are you *kidding* me?!" shouted Zoe. "Sam! What does our team name mean? THINK!"

For the first time Samuel actually looked embarrassed. He refused to make eye contact with his team, staring instead at the ground. "It's a stupid name anyway."

"Stupid or not," said Jake, "I'm afraid you guys have lost this time around. Kwam Gla, congratulations. With your prize I think you'll be sleeping a little more soundly tonight."

He began to unload big, fluffy pillows from the back of a nearby truck, handing one to each of the Kwam Gla members. Kwam Gla whooped and hugged their pillows while Pom Likit watched. Samuel stalked off. Unlike when Brenna had disappeared, no one went to look for him.

To continue, turn to page 34.

"Welcome back, teams," said Jake two days later. "I hope you've further adapted to island living."

"I still hate crab," Peter mumbled under his breath.

"And he never hesitates to tell us that," said Hannah.

"Pom Likit?" Jake asked. "Are you guys getting along?"

"For the most part," said Zoe. "But this is a competition. We're not all supposed to be best friends."

"That's for sure," said Samuel.

"It was nice to have Immunity, though," said Randy.

"Speaking of Immunity," said Jake, "I'll need to take this back from you guys." He walked over to retrieve the Immunity idol from Pom Likit. Zoe reluctantly handed it to him.

"Your next Immunity Challenge will involve something I'm sure you've all become familiar with since you arrived . . . coconuts."

If you want the tribes to play basketball in their challenge, turn to page 35.
If you want the tribes to go bowling in their challenge, turn to page 37.

"The name of your next challenge is 'I'm Going *Coco*nuts,' and in this one you'll be playing basketball," Jake said, motioning to two trees behind him where nets had been hung. "But first you'll have to get your own basketballs. That's where the coconuts come in.

"You guys are all going to have to find your own coconuts. Once you do, you can come back here and start shooting baskets. First team to get forty baskets wins."

"I'll rule at this," said Peter. "I'm the captain of my basketball team at home!"

"Keep in mind," said Jake, "that each team member has to score at least five points. But that will only bring you to twenty points. The remaining points are wild in terms of who scores them."

Peter looked around at his teammates. "Just let me score the extra points, okay?"

April, Carlos, and Hannah nodded. They knew they may as well let Peter do some work for a change.

"Also," added Jake, turning to Pom Likit, "to make the teams even, one of you will have to sit out."

"I'll do it," Samuel volunteered. "You guys will be better off; I really stink at basketball."

"Thanks, Sam," said Zoe. "That was considerate."

"Surprised?" said Samuel, making a face.

At the whistle's blow, the eight players ran toward a nearby thatch of trees. They shimmied up them and secured coconuts. Then they ran back and started throwing, each team at its own basket.

"One at a time, guys!" yelled Jake.

The competitors lined up and took turns throwing the

coconuts. Each team member was allowed only one toss before returning to the end of the line. Kwam Gla took an early lead due to Peter's impeccable shooting skills. But the rest of the team members proved to be pretty decent shooters as well.

"April," yelled Peter. "Stop shooting underhand."

April sunk another basket and yelled back, "Why do you even care, as long as it's working?"

Peter just scowled and threw another coconut, which sailed through the center of the basket.

Pom Likit, on the other hand, was having some problems. Brenna was not making any baskets, and she finally gave up.

"I can't do it!" she yelled. "I don't care about this stupid game anymore, I just want to go home." She ran off, with Lily taking off after her. Randy and Zoe continued to take turns shooting.

A few seconds later Kwam Gla sunk their fortieth basket to Pom Likit's twenty-nine.

"Congratulations, Kwam Gla!" announced Jake. "You've won Immunity." He started to hand the Immunity idol to April, but Peter snatched it away before she could take it.

Zoe, Randy, and Samuel left to catch up with Lily and Brenna.

To return to Pom Likit's camp before Tribal Council, turn to page 39.
To go straight to Tribal Council, turn to page 40.

"Okay," Jake continued. "How many of you have been bowling?"

All nine Survivors raised their hands.

"Good," said Jake. "So you'll be on equal ground."

"I didn't say I was any good!" said Hannah.

Jake rolled a coconut to each of the nine players. "Welcome to 'Coconut Bowl.' Come with me."

Each player picked up a coconut and followed Jake down the beach until they came across a makeshift bowling alley, with two lanes and pins made out of bamboo.

Jake set each team up with an alley. "First team to knock down two hundred and fifty pins wins Immunity. Each member must knock down at least forty pins. The rest are up for grabs. Each player will get two rolls each turn, just like in real bowling. I'll be keeping score. A member of our crew will help out by picking up pins.

"And one last thing. To make the teams even, a Pom Likit member will have to sit out. Any volunteers?"

Brenna came forward. "Bowling was never my favorite game," she said.

The remaining members of Pom Likit smiled gratefully at her.

The teams decided on a bowling order and took a few practice rolls. Then the whistle blew, and they started bowling for real. Pom Likit got off to an early lead due to Randy's supreme bowling skills, but Kwam Gla was never far behind. Then Zoe started having trouble, throwing gutter after gutter. Since she'd only knocked down twenty-six pins, the team now relied on her to get her remaining fourteen.

"Come on, Zoe," said Samuel. "Just picture my face on those pins."

Zoe burst out laughing as Kwam Gla caught up to their score and showed no signs of stopping. Zoe succeeded in knocking three pins down.

Then it was Lily against Carlos. Each needed to get either a spare or a strike to win the challenge for their team.

Lily rolled and knocked down seven. Carlos knocked down eight.

"Just three more, Lily!" yelled Zoe.

"Come on, Carlos, you can do it!" screamed April.

Each player took their shot . . . and Lily's coconut rolled right into the gutter. Carlos, on the other hand, knocked his remaining two pins down. His teammates engulfed him, cheering.

"Nice job, Kwam Gla," said Jake. "This time, Immunity is yours." He handed the Immunity idol to Carlos, who had eagerly run up to grab it while April and Hannah rolled their eyes in the background.

Jake turned to look at Pom Likit. "I'll see you guys tonight at Tribal Council."

To return to Pom Likit's camp before Tribal Council, turn to page 39.
To go straight to Tribal Council, turn to page 40.

Lily approached Randy and Zoe, who were boiling crab for dinner.

"Hey guys," she said. "Can we talk about Tribal Council?"

"Sure," said Randy. "What's up?"

"I think it's best to send Brenna home," said Lily. "As much as I like her, she's really homesick, and I don't think she'd be helping us if she stayed on."

"No way," said Zoe. "I say we form an alliance and send Sam back to his books. He's too smart, and that's dangerous to the rest of us."

Lily looked back toward the entrance of the cave, where Samuel was pouring coconut milk into a bucket while Brenna sat off to the side, her head on her knees. She looked miserable. Lily looked back at Randy.

"What do you think?" she asked him.

Randy shrugged. "I'm not sure yet. I still have to think about it."

"Always a diplomat," said Zoe, shaking her head.

"Not really," said Randy. "Just playing the game."

To continue, turn to page 40.

The members of Pom Likit slowly made their way to the Tribal Council site.

"Hey guys," Jake greeted them. "How are you feeling?"

Samuel scowled at him. "What kind of a question is that? How do you think?"

"Why don't you tell us how you *really* feel, Sam," Zoe said sarcastically.

"You have every right to be nervous," said Jake. "One of you will be going home tonight. But that means that four of you will be staying, so overall, your odds are still pretty good."

"Thanks," said Samuel. "I feel *much* better now."

"I'm going to hand out slips of paper," Jake said. "Each of you will have a chance to approach the urn, where you'll find a pen to write your vote with. After you vote, fold up the paper and put it in the urn. All voting is strictly confidential, and when you're done, I'll read out the votes. Majority rules. Any questions?"

The team shook their heads.

"Then let's begin," said Jake. "Lily, why don't you start?"

A few minutes later all five had cast their votes. Jake got the urn and placed it in front of them. He took the first piece of paper out.

"Brenna," he said, holding it up. Then he unwrapped the next one. "Sam," he said. Then it was one more for Brenna. And another for Sam.

Samuel clenched and unclenched his fists in anticipation. Jake unfurled the final slip of paper and held it up.

"Brenna," he announced, and Samuel cheered. Lily and Zoe glared at him.

But Brenna looked relieved as she walked up to Jake and handed him her torch.

"The tribe has spoken," Jake said to Brenna. "And you don't look too upset about that!"

Brenna turned to hug her teammates—even Samuel—good-bye. She smiled weakly. "I guess I'm not Survivor material."

To see what happened the next morning at
Kwam Gla's camp, turn to page 42.
To see what happened the next morning at
Pom Likit's camp, turn to page 43.
To go straight to the next Reward Challenge,
turn to page 44.

Carlos woke up his teammates by swinging on a vine outside their shelter and hollering.

"Hey, Tarzan!" shouted Peter. He went up to Carlos. "Let's talk."

"About what?" asked Carlos.

Peter put his arm around him. "I think you and I should think about forming an alliance. I've been having some trouble seeing eye to eye with Hannah, and I think she's just getting in our way."

Carlos shrugged. "I don't know, Peter. I like Hannah and April. They're organized."

"They're bossy," said Peter. "Look, do what you want. I just have a feeling they're forming an alliance, and I'm just trying to think ahead."

"I'll think about it," said Carlos. Then he sprinted off into the jungle. When he returned, he noticed April and Hannah huddled by the shelter. Could Peter have been right?

To continue, turn to page 44.

The four remaining players sat outside the cave eating pineapple and coconut for breakfast. They'd been quiet since sending Brenna home. However, none of them had forgotten that they were still there to win a game. Zoe decided to take a swim, and Samuel took advantage of her absence to talk to Lily and Randy.

"I think we need to watch out for Zoe's temper," he said. "I'm not sure I completely trust her."

"Well, ultimately, we're all here to win," said Randy.

"Besides," said Lily. "You have a temper too."

Samuel rolled his eyes. "We can't all do yoga to keep us calm, Lily. Anyway, I just wanted to bring it up. You never can tell what people are really thinking, so I wanted to try and start an honest conversation."

"Well," said Lily. "Let me know when you're ready to have one. An honest conversation, that is."

She walked off toward the water. Randy looked at Samuel and shrugged.

"Time for a new plan," Samuel muttered to himself.

To continue, turn to page 44.

"So," said Jake as the Survivors gathered for their next challenge. "How are you guys at rock climbing?"

"Dude, are you serious?" said Peter. "I love it."

"Me too," said Randy. "I'm from Colorado, and rock climbing is, like, my middle name."

"All right, then," said Jake. "Looks like we'll have a solid competition. Now. What about gymnastics?"

"I've taken gymnastics and dance since I was three," said Lily. "No problem."

"Great," said Jake. "Your next activity is called 'Rock and Roll.' The first part involves some rock, as in rock climbing. And the second part is all about rolling, as in tumbling on those mats over there. Each of you will need to scale that rock." He pointed behind him to a rock about thirty feet high. "We'll be spotting you and monitoring your equipment. Once you've completed that, you'll need to tumble your way—one at a time—down that mat." He pointed to a long blue mat rolled out beneath the rock. "When I say tumble, I mean a head over heels somersault. If any of you don't know how to either rock or roll, I advise you to use the next fifteen minutes to learn how. Good luck."

If you want Kwam Gla to win the reward, turn to page 45.
If you want Pom Likit to win the reward, turn to page 46.

Peter had wanted to go first, but the others convinced him that they needed his skills at the end. Instead Carlos went first against Lily for Pom Likit.

They were neck and neck—both small, and able to lift themselves relatively easily.

Next came Zoe and Hannah, who were also evenly matched. Then Samuel and April. Samuel was surprisingly good against April, but had some trouble getting a foothold toward the top, giving April a slight lead.

Peter took advantage of the lead and, after fastening himself into the climbing gear, started climbing aggressively. Samuel had finished for Pom Likit, and Randy was gaining on Peter. Peter increased his speed, but his foot kept slipping.

"Peter," yelled Hannah. "Just take it easy."

"I know what I'm doing!" shouted Peter.

Randy started to pass him on the rock, but Peter took a deep breath and was able to get his bearings again. The two were neck and neck, reaching the top at the same time and then gliding down almost in unison.

At the bottom the teams raced to tumble down the mats one at a time. It was close, but Kwam Gla was able to finish first. They were psyched to discover that their prize was a movie screening with popcorn and soda!

"You're a really good climber," said Hannah. "But you didn't need to be so macho. It just got in your way."

"We won, didn't we, Hannah?" Peter said.

To continue, turn to page 48.

Both teams started out strong on the rocks. The last person up for Pom Likit was Zoe, and for Kwam Gla, Carlos.

"Hey, Zoe!" yelled Randy. "Last time I checked, there weren't too many rocks to climb in New York City. How come you're so good at this?"

"You know, they do have indoor climbing walls in New York," Zoe answered. "And it just so happens that I go all the time."

Meanwhile Carlos was struggling on the rock. "Carlos, move to the right," Hannah instructed. "Okay, now—"

"You don't have to do everything she says, Carlos," yelled Peter. "Just go with your gut. You have to trust your own strength."

Hannah ignored Peter. "Carlos, if you just bring your right foot up a few inches, there's a crevice there."

Carlos moved his foot and found the spot Hannah had pointed out. Feeling more secure, he reached up for a new hold and was able to scramble up the remaining few feet. He then started rappelling down.

All four members of Pom Likit had successfully scaled and rappelled, and they were now starting to roll.

"Come on, Carlos!" Peter yelled as he paced back and forth. "Move faster! They're winning!"

"Real smooth," said April. "It's okay, Carlos; you're almost there."

But by the time he hit the ground, Pom Likit was already halfway done with their tumbling. Randy and Zoe had finished and were cheering on Lily, who was quickly somersaulting her way down the mat.

April began flipping and caught up to Lily. Then Samuel was pitted against Carlos. Carlos, much smaller than Samuel, was able to reach the end by the time Samuel had only done a few awkward tumbles. Kwam Gla started getting hopeful again.

Unfortunately, even though Peter was able to finish just ahead of Samuel, there was no way that Hannah could finish before him. Pom Likit won, but barely. Even faced with a loss, Kwam Gla felt energized that they had been able to pull together so quickly.

"Okay, Pom Likit," said Jake. "This is your lucky day. Today's prize is a movie screening with popcorn and soda."

Kwam Gla's energy quickly dissolved when they saw Pom Likit celebrating.

"Oh well," said April. "Popcorn and soda are really fattening anyway."

Carlos, Peter, and Hannah looked at her.

"Dude," said Hannah. "At this point, I'm sick of the Survivor starvation diet. Enough with the boiled crab and coconut."

"Quit whining," said Peter. "We'll get 'em next time."

To continue, turn to page 48.

"So," Jake asked before the teams started their third Immunity Challenge. "How are you guys holding up?"

"We're doing well," Samuel said. "I think we've all adjusted and, for the most part, are getting along."

Zoe rolled her eyes.

"Zoe?" Jake asked. "Do you not agree with Sam?"

"It's not that I disagree with him," said Zoe. "I just don't trust him."

"I know what she's talking about," said April. "Like we're supposed to be looking out for ourselves, right? But we have to spend so much time together and rely on each other to get by."

Jake nodded. "You're right. It's a tough situation." He took a pause. "Kwam Gla, I'm afraid I'll need the Immunity idol back."

April walked up to Jake and handed the clay figure over.

"Thanks," said Jake. "Okay, now back to today's challenge."

If you want the tribes to play the challenge on land, turn to page 49.
If you want the tribes to play the challenge in the water, turn to page 51.

"This challenge is called 'Get on My Back,'" said Jake. "It's a race in which you'll go completely around the island. We've set up twenty flags in different places, ten for each team. Pom Likit, your flags are blue, and Kwam Gla, yours are green. The first team to gather all their flags wins."

"How do we know where to find them?" asked Zoe.

"Ah, good question," said Jake. "On each flag will be the information as to where the next flag is located. It's pretty straightforward—no tricks or clues you need to decipher. But there *is* one thing: Someone must be carried on someone else's back at all times. You can make one switch, but that's it.

"Take the next five minutes to figure out who you want to be carried and who wants to do the carrying."

The choices weren't that difficult to make: Lily for Pom Likit and Carlos for Kwam Gla. They were the smallest players and would be the easiest to transport.

"See, Carlos?" said Hannah. "Being small can have its rewards."

"I'll start off carrying Carlos," said Peter.

"And I've got Lily to start," said Randy.

True to Jake's word, the flags weren't hard to find. However, Kwam Gla ran into some trouble when Peter tired of carrying Carlos.

"I need one of you to take over," he said, hunched over with a cramp in his side.

"Don't look at me," said Hannah. "I have a really bad back. I hurt it playing field hockey last year."

"Well," said April, "In that case I guess it's on me,

then. Literally. Come on, Carlos. Let's go!"

Carlos hopped onto April's back, but unfortunately he was heavier than he looked, and she soon tired of the extra weight. Kwam Gla ultimately had to forfeit the round.

Randy, who was much taller than Lily, had no problem carrying her for most of the race, with Samuel holding her for the last two flags. Pom Likit was victorious and relieved they didn't have to return to the council.

"Nice work, Pom Likit," said Jake when both teams had assembled back at the meeting site. He looked at Kwam Gla. "Looks like you guys will be making a return visit to Tribal Council. I'll see you there."

"Great," Hannah said sarcastically. "Looking forward to it."

To return to Kwam Gla's camp before Tribal
Council, turn to page 53.
To go straight to Tribal Council, turn to page 54.

"This challenge," Jake said, "is called 'Swim for Immunity.' It's a relay race. Sounds simple enough, right? Wrong. This relay race is also an aqua race. We've set up two stakes out in the water with four flags on each. Each team member needs to swim out to the post and grab a flag. Red flags are Kwam Gla's and yellow are Pom Likit's. First team to collect all four flags wins Immunity."

The members of Pom Likit looked around at one another nervously.

"Are you going to be okay with this, Zoe?" asked Randy. Zoe looked concerned, but tried to cover it.

"I'll be fine, guys," she said. Then she turned to Jake. "Can I use my inner tube for this one?" she asked, then added, "I'm kidding," after noticing her teammates' worried looks.

The team huddled. "You can do it, Zoe," said Lily. "Don't worry about us. Don't worry about winning. Just concentrate on getting to the flag however you need to get there."

Over in the Kwam Gla huddle, the foursome compared swimming skills.

"I love to swim," said Carlos.

"Yeah, no problems here," said Hannah.

"My older sister is a lifeguard," said April. "We totally live at the pool in the summer." She looked at Peter. "How about you?"

Peter shrugged. "I'll be fine."

"Are you a good swimmer?" asked Hannah.

"I said, I'll be fine!" Peter answered.

However, for all of Peter's insistence that he would

be "fine," he wasn't. When pitted against Zoe, she was able to pull ahead simply because her team was behind her. They cheered her on as she made her way slowly out to the post, grabbed the flag, and then passed Peter on her way back in to shore.

"Congratulations, Pom Likit," said Jake. "You've escaped Tribal Council this time around." He looked at the members of Kwam Gla. "I'll see you four tonight."

Peter stalked off toward camp, not bothering to wait for anyone else.

To return to Kwam Gla's camp before Tribal Council, turn to page 53.

To go straight to Tribal Council, turn to page 54.

"You've changed your mind about Peter, right?" Hannah asked April as they took a walk later that afternoon. "I mean, he's totally rude and gets in our way."

"Yeah," said April. "And he's not even as good an athlete as he says he is. He's no good in the water."

"We have to talk to Carlos and convince him that he needs to vote with us," said Hannah.

Just then they heard some rustling above them. They looked up just in time to see Carlos jump down from a tree, two coconuts in his hands.

"You guys should really be more careful where you talk about forming alliances," he said, smirking.

"Whoops," said Hannah. "So. Are you with us?"

Carlos shrugged. "Maybe. I need to think about it."

"Carlos!" called Peter from camp. "Get back here now."

"Bossy, isn't he?" asked April.

Again Carlos shrugged, walking back toward camp. "I'll see you guys later."

Hannah and April watched him walk away, perplexed.

"Carlos could turn out to be more clever than I thought," said Hannah. "He may even be playing all of us."

To continue, turn to page 54.

That evening April, Hannah, Carlos, and Peter left their camp to vote another teammate off the island.

"Welcome back," said Jake. "What's up?"

"I don't want to go home," said Carlos.

"Do you have any reason to think you could be headed there?" asked Jake.

Carlos looked around at his teammates. "I don't know," he said. "Do I?"

No one replied. They all just looked straight ahead.

One by one the votes were dropped into the urn. Jake retrieved them and started to read them aloud.

"One for Peter," he said. Peter frowned. Jake unrolled another. "And one for Hannah."

Hannah looked surprised, but then glared at Peter.

"Another for Peter," Jake read, pausing before unfolding the last slip of paper. He turned the paper around so that Kwam Gla could know their fate.

It said "Peter."

Peter sneered at the remaining members of Kwam Gla as he went up to Jake. "You guys will see," he said. "I'm the only one who was really trying to win this thing. It's a game . . . and you *all* can't survive."

"The tribe has spoken," said Jake, snuffing out Peter's torch. "It's time to go."

Before they went to sleep, the three remaining Kwam Gla tribe members sat around a campfire, drinking tea made from some berries. April's interest in the environment and love of camping had repeatedly come in handy: She knew what was edible and how to prepare it.

"Y'know," said Hannah. "Even though I don't like

Peter, it's still hard to see a person get voted off."

"I thought you were so gung ho to see him get sent home," said Carlos. "You're the one who helped convince me to vote for him."

"Yeah, I know," said Hannah. "You're right. Enough with the guilt."

"I wonder who's next," said April.

"We don't need to think about it tonight," said Hannah. "Let's just chill out."

"Done," said April.

Meanwhile, over at Pom Likit's campsite, Samuel and Randy played chess while Lily and Zoe looked at pictures. Samuel had brought a portable chess set as his luxury item while Lily had brought a photo album with pictures of all her friends and family back in Hawaii.

"So, have you thought at all about what we talked about?" Samuel asked Randy. They were out of earshot of the girls.

"What do you mean?" said Randy.

"About forming an alliance," said Samuel. "I think Zoe is strong. She's a threat to all of us. I say she goes next if we lose Immunity."

Randy shrugged. "I'm not much for alliances."

"Randy, don't be stupid," said Samuel. "No one can trust anyone here. But by forming an alliance, at least we can take each other to the end of the game."

"Well, you tell me how that works out for you," said Randy. He moved a piece on the board. "Checkmate."

To continue, turn to page 56.

The next morning Jake rode up to the meeting place in a canoe. The seven remaining tribe members—three from Kwam Gla and four from Pom Likit—met him in the water and helped to pull the boat ashore.

Behind him, two long canoes were being steered in, each one with room for four people.

"Are those for us?" asked Lily.

"You got it," said Jake as he hopped out of the canoe and staked a paddle in the sand. "Your next Reward Challenge is called 'Canoe Help Me?'. And you guys are going to get quite a workout from it. Are you up for the challenge?"

The group nodded.

"Bring it on!" said Zoe.

"The ultimate goal is to complete a puzzle," Jake continued. "The final picture is of a reticulated python, which is the longest snake in the world—reaching up to twenty-six feet. It's been known to reside on this island."

"WHAT?" asked Zoe. "*Why* did you have to tell us that?"

Jake smiled. "Don't worry, Zoe. We obviously don't have you guys set up near any pythons. But it's still wise to know what they look like, and to respect their power."

"No problem with that," said Zoe. "Just keep 'em far, far away."

"Each team will have to canoe to different locations to retrieve a total of nine puzzle pieces. Once you have them all, you need to return to this spot and assemble them until you finish the puzzle. Any questions?"

Everyone shook their heads.

"Okay, then," said Jake. "There's just one more thing. To make the teams even, one of the Pom Likit members will have to sit out."

"I'll do it," said Zoe. "Since I'm not at my best in the water."

"Are you sure?" asked Randy.

She nodded. "Yeah. I'll just cheer you guys on from the beach."

"Thanks, Zoe," Jake said. "Okay teams, you have ten minutes to familiarize yourself with the canoes. Then we'll set you off to your first destination."

If you want Pom Likit to win the reward, turn to page 58.
If you want Kwam Gla to win the reward, turn to page 60.

Pom Likit got off to a strong start due to Lily and Randy's familiarity with the water—Lily from living in Hawaii and Randy from white-water river rafting on vacations with his family every year. They had no problem getting from one spot to the next; even Samuel was surprisingly agreeable.

Meanwhile Kwam Gla fought to finish the race. Carlos had accidentally lost one of the paddles overboard after the third piece was attained, so he, Hannah, and April had had to make do with only one paddle for the remainder of the race.

By the time Pom Likit had retrieved all nine pieces, they had a comfortable lead over Kwam Gla, who was still stuck at only five pieces. Lily, Randy, and Samuel worked swiftly to assemble the puzzle, and when they were done, Zoe—from her place on the sidelines—smiled at their handiwork.

"I never thought I'd be so happy to see a snake!" she said.

Kwam Gla finally got all nine pieces and tiredly began assembling their puzzle.

"Come on over here, guys," said Jake when they were done. "You all did fine." He turned to Pom Likit. "Are you ready for your prize?"

"Totally," said Randy.

"Well," said Jake, "I'm sure you guys are beginning to really miss talking to certain people . . . your friends, your family. We've set it up so that each of you will get to make an hour-long phone call to the person of your choice."

"Even me?" said Zoe. "I mean, I didn't step foot in a canoe."

Jake nodded. "Even you, Zoe."

"That rocks!" said Zoe.

The members of Kwam Gla walked slowly back to their camp.

"That prize would have been nice to have," Hannah said.

"I know," said April. "I miss talking to my best friend."

"Too bad you had to ruin it," Hannah said to Carlos.

"Hey," said Carlos. "Everyone makes mistakes."

"Let's try and keep the mistakes to a minimum from now on," said Hannah as she sprinted ahead.

Carlos looked at April. "What was that all about?"

April looked after Hannah. "Not sure. She's probably just bummed about not getting that phone call."

"Yeah, well," said Carlos. "I thought we sent the biggest jerk on this team home already."

April was silent as they continued walking toward camp.

To continue, turn to page 61.

April, Hannah, and Carlos worked well together, switching off who rowed and who held the puzzle pieces that they found. They quickly collected all nine pieces and paddled back to shore to put together the puzzle.

Zoe cheered Pom Likit on from the shore as they paddled out, but they were not having the same luck as Kwam Gla. Lily and Randy were getting along, while Samuel was causing problems. He insisted on taking a paddle but couldn't steer straight. He kept sending them backward, farther away from their goal. Then he capsized the canoe, throwing everyone into the water!

"Sam!" screamed Lily.

"Just get back into the canoe," said Randy. "We don't have time to lose."

With Randy and Lily steering, they got back on track, but it was too late. By the time they got the ninth piece, Kwam Gla had finished assembling the puzzle, which showed a huge python, fangs gleaming.

"Nice job, Kwam Gla," said Jake. "You guys will be happy to hear that you're now entitled to an hour-long phone call with the person of your choice."

"I'm calling my mom!" said Hannah.

"I'm calling my best friend," said April.

"Hmm," said Carlos. "If you guys give me your phone calls, I'll clean camp for a week."

The girls shook their heads.

"I have news for you, Carlos," said April. "You're still expected to help clean the camp!"

To continue, turn to page 61.

"Hi, guys. We're up to the fourth Immunity Challenge," said Jake as the remainder of both tribes approached the meeting place. "It's time for me to take back the idol."

Zoe walked up and handed it to Jake.

"Now, this next challenge is called 'Scavengers,'" continued Jake. "How many of you have gone on a scavenger hunt?"

All seven players raised their hands.

"Good," said Jake. "So you know the basic idea. Each team will get a list of objects to find. Some of these objects are native to the island. Some of them are not; we've just planted them somewhere. The first team to collect all of the items wins Immunity this time around. Here are two baskets, one for each team."

He handed one basket to April and one to Lily.

"Once again, someone from Pom Likit will have to sit this one out. Any volunteers?"

Randy looked up. "I think it's my turn," he said. "I'll sit this one out."

"Thanks, Randy," said Jake. He looked at the remaining six players. "Ready to begin? Let's go."

The six Survivors got their lists and split up by team. Kwam Gla walked off in the direction of their camp. Pom Likit set off into the jungle, studying their list along the way.

"One iPod, a container of coconut milk, a stuffed manatee, three oysters, a pair of 'lucky' sneakers, and a leaf from the tontaperdagi plant," Sam read out loud.

"Where are we going to find an iPod on this island?" asked Lily.

"I have no idea," said Zoe. "Did either one of you bring this as your luxury item?" she asked.

Both Lily and Samuel shook their heads 'no'.

"Well, neither did I," Zoe said. "What about 'lucky' sneakers?" she asked hopefully.

"I have sneakers," said Lily, "but what do they mean by 'lucky'?" she said.

"They are obviously referring to a specific pair of sneakers, but whose: that is the question," Sam remarked.

"And what's a tontaperdagi plant?" asked Zoe.

"I know," said Lily. "Remember, at the beginning Jake told us about some of the plants on the island?"

The others shrugged.

"Anyway, I think I remember what this one looked like. It has edible red fruit on it. Look, we've already spent a lot of time talking. Let's go off and find the food and the plant leaf first, and then we can worry about the other stuff. We don't have any more time to waste. Let's go!"

Meanwhile, Kwam Gla was huddling near their campsite, discussing their strategy.

"Okay," said Carlos. "Come on, guys—we need to focus if we want to win this thing. And we need to win this challenge. We can't afford to lose Immunity again."

"You're right," said Hannah.

"Two palm fronds, some taro root, clams, grubs," April read aloud. "This shouldn't be too hard."

"Wait a second," said Hannah. "A photo album? A

Yankees cap? A chess set? What is this? Where are we going to find these things?"

"I think that girl Zoe is from New York," said Carlos. "She might like the Yankees."

"Carlos, you're a genius!" said April. "This stuff belongs to Pom Likit. We have their three luxury items on our list. We need to sneak into their camp and retrieve them."

"Shouldn't be too hard, since they'll be busy looking for the stuff on their list," said Carlos.

"Wait a second," said Hannah. "If we have stuff of theirs on our list, then most likely our stuff is on their list, right?"

"Yeah," said April. "So?"

"So," continued Hannah. "Why don't we go and grab our stuff, so they won't be able to find it?"

"Wow, that's pretty sneaky," said April. She smiled. "I love it! Let's go kick some Pom Likit butt!" said April.

The three of them went to grab their luxury items: April's stuffed manatee, Hannah's iPod, and Carlos's "lucky" sneakers. Then they headed to Pom Likit's camp to find the three luxury items on their own list.

"Okay," said Hannah, "April, you look for the Yankees cap. Carlos, you find the chess set, and I'll look for the photo album."

"Got it!" yelled Carlos. "Ha! Left it right out in the open. Looks like he was in the middle of a game, too."

"Shhhh . . ." whispered Hannah. "We have to be quiet in case they come back."

Just then Hannah spotted Lily's photo album. She

turned to April, who was still searching for Zoe's Yankees cap. Hannah and Sam pitched in and helped April look for it.

"Got it," said April. "She must really love it because she sleeps with it inside her mat. Okay, hurry, let's get out of here."

A few minutes later, Kwam Gla had left Pom Likit's camp with Zoe's Yankees cap, Sam's chess set, and Lily's photo album in hand. Then they made their way into the jungle to search for the remaining items on their list. Right then, Pom Likit came out of the jungle with three oysters, a container of coconut milk, and a leaf from the tontaperdagi plant. They retreated back to their campsite to discuss where the other three items could be.

"I'm so grateful that you're here," Zoe said to Lily. "You know where things are on the island."

"Yeah, so where are we going to find an iPod, a stuffed manatee, and 'lucky' sneakers?" asked Samuel.

"Well," said Lily, "these are things that are not naturally found on the island, so they must have been brought here by people."

"And if they weren't brought here by us," said Samuel, "they must have been brought here by members of the other team!"

"Which means," continued Sam, "that we must have their luxury items on our list."

"Wait a minute," said Zoe, "that means that they have our luxury items on their list. Quick, check if your stuff is still here!" she yelled.

"My chess set," screamed Sam, "it's gone!"

"So is my Yankees cap," said Zoe.

"And my photo album," cried Lily.

"I can't believe they took my chess set. Are they allowed to just come in here and steal our stuff like that?" Sam asked angrily.

"I'm sure you'll get it back, Sam. Stop complaining so much. It's not helping!" yelled Zoe.

"Whatever, Miss Oh-no-they-have-my-ratty-old-baseball-cap," said Samuel.

"Hey!" said Zoe. "That cap means a lot to me"

"Well," said Samuel, "so does my chess set."

"Guys!" Lily screamed. "Stop fighting! We don't have time for this. We have to get into Kwam Gla's camp and get the items that are on our list before we lose Immunity!"

"She's right," said Zoe.

The three of them ran off. A few minutes later the members of Pom Likit burst into Kwam Gla's camp looking for the luxury items they needed.

"I don't see them!" yelled Samuel.

"Calm down," said Lily. "They have to be here somewhere."

"No," said Zoe. "Sam's right. They're not here."

"Shhhh. Guys, listen!" cried Lily.

The three of them paused. They heard cheering off in the distance. Kwam Gla had found all of the items on their list! They had outsmarted Pom Likit and won the challenge.

"Looks like we're out of luck," said Samuel. He sat down, placing the basket with the items they'd collected so far beside him.

"Sam," said Zoe. "We still need to finish."

"Why?" he asked. "What's the point?"

"The point is," said Lily, "we're playing a game, and we need to finish it. Otherwise we're quitters, and I don't want to be a quitter. I don't want to look like a sore loser."

"Come on, Lily," said Zoe, picking up the basket.

"Let's go." She turned back to Samuel. "You're welcome to join us. We'll do our best to get your chess set back."

Samuel eventually got up and followed the other two. But he knew that they were headed to Tribal Council that evening, and he was already feeling defeated.

To return to Pom Likit's campsite before Tribal Council, turn to page 67.

To go straight to Tribal Council, turn to page 68.

"Can I talk to you two?" Samuel asked Lily and Randy later that day. Zoe was taking a swim down at the beach.

"Sure," Randy said, taking a break from collecting dry twigs for a campfire.

"Well," said Samuel, "I was thinking that it might be smart to form an alliance."

"I told you already," said Randy, "I'm not interested."

"And I told you," said Samuel, "that I think it's stupid not to."

"I assume you want to get rid of Zoe," said Lily.

Samuel nodded. "Yeah. I don't think she pulls her weight around here. And she *never* shuts up."

"I think Zoe's an asset to the team," Randy said.

"Lily?" asked Samuel. "What about you?"

"I'm not really into alliances," said Lily.

"Fine," said Samuel. "Do what you want. I know what I need to do to protect myself." He walked away.

Little did Samuel know that Lily had already formed a pact with Zoe, and they both planned on voting Samuel off that night.

To continue, turn to page 68.

"Come on down," said Jake to the four remaining members of Pom Likit. He noticed that Samuel looked especially nervous.

"Sam?" asked Jake. "How are you?"

"Fine," Samuel said defensively. "Why?"

"Just checking in," said Jake. "Okay. Are you ready to cast your votes?"

Four heads nodded. One by one they made their way to the urn and placed their votes inside. Jake retrieved the urn and proceeded to read the ballots aloud.

"One vote for Sam," said Jake, unfurling the first piece of paper he chose. "And one for Zoe."

Zoe tried making eye contact with Samuel, but he wouldn't look her way. Jake unwrapped another piece of paper.

"Another for Sam," he said. Then he paused before saying, "This could go in two directions. We could either have a tie, or . . . well, we'll see."

Samuel clenched his fists as Jake took out the final slip of paper. Jake looked down at it before turning it around so the team could see. It said in big, block letters: SAM.

Samuel exhaled slowly. Then he got up and walked over to Jake, tipping in his torch to be extinguished.

"Good game," said Jake. "But the tribe has spoken."

"Yeah," said Samuel. He turned around to face his team one last time and then walked off.

To continue, turn to page 69.

Two days later the two teams gathered by a running stream deep in the jungle for their next Reward Challenge.

"You've all seen some of the monkeys on the island," said Jake. "In 'Monkey See, Monkey Do' you'll need to *do* what the monkeys do."

"Eat our food and steal our stuff?" said Randy with a smirk.

"Not quite," said Jake. "This challenge involves swinging on a vine across a stream. There are flags buried on either side of the stream; the first team to collect ten wins. Only catch is, after you uncover each flag, you need to swing back to the other side. Each teammate has to be involved, and no one can swing more than one time in a row.

"Anyone interested to know what you're playing for?" asked Jake.

The competitors nodded yes.

"Let's just say I hope you brought shoes you can dance in," said Jake. "And I hope you like cheeseburgers. And pizza."

Zoe turned toward her teammates and said, "We *so* have to win this!"

If you want Pom Likit to win the reward, turn to page 70.
If you want Kwam Gla to win the reward, turn to page 71.

Jake took his place between two vines before saying, "On your mark . . . get set . . . GO!"

Lily swung first for Pom Likit, quickly uncovering the first orange flag in a mound of bamboo, leaves, and dirt. She was pitted against Carlos, who also managed to find the flag quickly. Then it was Randy against Hannah. Randy was strong on the rope, while it took Hannah a few tries to get across to the other side. Zoe then swung against April, and it was no contest. While April was a good athlete, she couldn't match Zoe on the rope. Pom Likit pulled ahead and maintained their lead until they retrieved all ten flags.

"Congratulations," said Jake to the three winners. "How do you guys feel about dancing?"

"Love it," said Lily.

"And how do you feel about pizza?"

"Love it even more," said Zoe.

"Then you're going to love your prize," said Jake. "Tonight there will be a party in your honor, with a DJ and all your favorite foods. And . . . you have the opportunity to extend an invitation to Kwam Gla—if you so desire."

Pom Likit didn't have to take too long to decide that's exactly what they wanted to do.

For a dance challenge, turn to page 72.
For a race challenge, turn to page 74.

"Okay, Carlos," said Hannah. "You're our secret weapon."

"Why?" said Carlos.

"Because you're fast," said Hannah. "And you're light. You'll have no trouble swinging on that vine."

"She's right," said April. "Now me, I'm not so sure."

"You'll be fine too," said Hannah. "I'm nervous that I won't be strong enough to hold on to the rope."

Jake raised his arms for silence. "On your mark," he said. "Get set . . . GO!"

Kwam Gla started out strong. Each member swung confidently, quickly uncovering the flags. Pom Likit started out in good shape, but then Randy dropped one of the flags. He had to travel down the ditch into the water to get it, leaving Kwam Gla to take the lead and win the challenge.

"Good job, guys," said Jake. "Randy, tough break. But only one team can win the reward . . . or can they?"

"What do you mean?" asked Carlos. "We won, fair and square."

"Absolutely," said Jake. "You won. And you won big: Tonight there will be a party for you guys, with a DJ and amazing food. But don't you think a party with six people is a lot more fun than a party with three people?"

April smiled. "What if the winners invite—no offense—the losers to the party?"

"That would be a very nice thing to do," said Jake.

For a dance challenge, turn to page 72.
For a race challenge, turn to page 74.

That night part of the island was turned into party central. A DJ was set up, as well as all sorts of food from home, including pizza and burgers, candy, macaroni and cheese, and fried chicken. There was a huge TV where video games could be played, and a karaoke microphone. For over an hour, they had a blast.

Then Jake quieted things down. "Are you having a good time?"

Everyone cheered.

"Do you wanna dance?"

Again everyone responded in cheer.

"Good," said Jake. "Because that's what we're planning. Now that you've had a chance to pig out, it's time to work out. We're going to have a danceathon. Last person standing wins Immunity for their team."

Everyone looked at one another—so much for a night off.

"Ready?" asked Jake. He turned to the DJ. "You're on."

For the first twenty minutes everyone was fine. Lily and Carlos were especially good dancers. Unfortunately Carlos wasn't good at conserving his energy.

"I gotta sit down," he said, doing just that in the middle of the dance floor. Zoe was next, followed by Hannah and then Randy. April faced off against Lily. Each was having a bit of a hard time, dancing slower and slower. But each was also stubbornly holding on, not wanting the responsibility of a loss for her team.

"Come on, April," cheered Hannah and Carlos.

"Stay with it, Lily," yelled Zoe and Randy.

Finally, after another fifteen minutes, April began

breathing heavily as she clutched her side.

"I can't go anymore," she said. "My side is killing me . . . I'm sorry."

Hannah and Carlos hurried over and put their arms around her.

"It's okay," Hannah said. "Don't worry about it."

But as April watched Pom Likit hug one another, she felt awful.

To return to Kwam Gla's campsite before Tribal Council, turn to page 76.
To go straight to Tribal Council, turn to page 77.

"Have enough dancing last night?" asked Jake the next morning as the tribes gathered in the meeting place.

The night before had been a great party, with everything the kids missed from home: the snacks, the music, the video games. They had stayed up very late and were now completely exhausted.

"I know you guys are tired," said Jake. "And you probably just want to go back to sleep. But you're going to need to keep moving.

"Today's challenge is pretty straightforward. It's a relay race. One team member will start with a baton, and then have to pass it on to the next person, and so on. The race will start on land, and then continue into the water, where you'll repeat the process. You guys decide the order. Whichever team finishes the entire race first wins Immunity. Got it?"

The six nodded.

It was decided that April and Randy would go first, followed by Hannah and Zoe, and then Carlos and Lily.

"I'm really good at relays," said Carlos. "Don't worry—I can save you guys, if necessary."

Hannah looked annoyed. "Who said we needed to be saved?" she asked.

"I'm just offering to help," said Carlos. "No need for the attitude."

"Guys," said April. "Enough."

Jake handed a baton to April and one to Randy. "Take your places," he said as the six players assembled themselves. "On the count of three. . . . One. Two. THREE!"

The teams were neck and neck for the first part of the race. They then entered the water at the same time, with April outswimming Randy. Zoe, while not a strong swimmer, had been practicing with Lily, and was able to make up the difference against Hannah. Finally Lily and Carlos dove in, clutching their batons as they swam out to the buoy. While Carlos was a good swimmer, he was no match for Lily, who had learned to swim almost before she had learned to walk. Lily pulled ahead, winning the race for her team.

Randy and Zoe carried her out of the water, cheering. Carlos dragged himself out, head down. He had a bad feeling that he was going to be the next to go.

To return to Kwam Gla's campsite before Tribal Council, turn to page 76.
To go straight to Tribal Council, turn to page 77.

The members of Kwam Gla spent a tension-filled afternoon together. Carlos was unusually calm.

"What's up with him?" Hannah asked April.

April shrugged. "Maybe he's scared that he'll be voted off."

"Maybe?" asked Hannah. "I'd say it's a pretty sure thing, wouldn't you?"

"We'll see," said April cryptically.

"April," said Hannah, "he can't be relied on. He's not mature enough. I thought you and I had a deal."

"I said we'll see," said April. She headed off into the forest for a walk. She knew that Carlos might be less of a threat to her overall. People liked Hannah more than him. And as much as she liked Hannah as a friend, April knew that, ultimately, she wasn't on Koh Tarutao to make friends.

To continue, turn to page 77.

Later that night Kwam Gla filed in to the Tribal Council site, not making eye contact with one another or with Jake. "It's getting down to the wire, huh?" asked Jake.

The three members nodded.

"It is hard when your teammates are friends as well as competitors," Jake said. "But you all should feel good about making it this far. Ready to cast your votes?"

"Not really," said Carlos. "But we don't have a choice, do we?"

April, Hannah, and Carlos took their turns approaching the urn and casting their votes. Jake brought the urn up to where he stood and rested it on a wooden column. He took out the first slip.

"The first vote is for Carlos," he said.

Carlos didn't look surprised.

Jake unfurled the next slip. "And one vote for Hannah."

Hannah also didn't look surprised; she figured that Carlos would vote for her.

Jake removed the final slip of paper from the urn. "And the third and deciding vote is for . . . Hannah."

Hannah looked at April in shock before she walked quickly up to Jake so he could snuff out her flame.

"Hannah," said Jake. "It looks like the tribe has spoken."

"Sorry," April mouthed to Hannah. But Hannah just ignored her and stalked off.

The five remaining players met up with Jake the next morning.

"Congratulations," said Jake, "on making it to the final five. You've probably become used to competing as two teams. I hope none of you were too attached to that idea, because from now on, you're *all* teammates.

"The five of you will need to come up with a name for your new team. I expect to hear it by the next Reward Challenge, which is in two days. That gives you plenty of time to brainstorm."

Two days later the five teammates returned to the meeting place.

"Okay," Jake said. "From now on there will be only one winner for each challenge. The winner may or may not get to share his or her reward with someone, but in the Immunity Challenges, there can *only* be one winner. That means that only one of you will achieve Immunity from Tribal Council from now on.

"But before we get started, have you decided on a new name for your tribe?"

"Khwaam Samret," replied Zoe. "It means 'success!'"

"Nice choice," said Jake. Okay, for your next Reward Challenge, there are eighteen of these hidden around the island." He held up a wooden elephant that stood about six inches high. "A portion of the island has been roped in, and that's your playing ground. The person to find the most elephants wins the reward. You'll have exactly two hours to look for elephants. Everybody ready?"

The players nodded.

"Okay," said Jake. "Ready . . . set . . . GO!"

The players got to work: digging, running, searching. In the end Zoe was victorious with six elephants, followed by Randy with four, April and Lily with three each, and Carlos with two.

"Zoe, you have a choice of who to take with you for your reward," said Jake.

If you want Zoe to share her reward with Lily, turn to page 80.
If you want Zoe to share her reward with Randy, turn to page 82.

"Well," said Zoe. "Lily's been a good friend to me throughout the game, so I choose her."

"Thanks, Zoe!" said Lily as she ran over to Zoe to give her a hug.

"Are you two ready for some pampering?" asked Jake.

Both girls nodded excitedly.

"Because that's what you'll be getting. You'll be taken to a remote part of the island, where there are real bubble baths and real beds waiting for each of you. You can spend the rest of the day reading magazines, hanging out, whatever you want.

"While they are being pampered, the rest of you need to determine which camp you're going to stay in from now on and transport your stuff over there."

Lily and Zoe were taken away while April, Randy, and Carlos trudged back toward the camps. They quickly decided that Pom Likit's base was the place to be since it had the natural shelter of a cave. Kwam Gla's handmade shelter had never done a good job of keeping the rain completely out.

"A bubble bath sounds really good right about now," said April.

"And an actual bed?" said Randy. "I'm so jealous."

Carlos turned to April and said, "I never got the chance to thank you for keeping me here."

"I didn't do it for you, Carlos," said April. "You're cool and all, but I'm just playing the game."

"We *all* are," added Randy.

Meanwhile Lily and Zoe were enjoying their temporary visit with luxury. They laid out on beach chairs and were served cold lemonade and brownies.

"I could get used to this," said Zoe.

"Don't get too used to it," said Lily.

"I know," said Zoe. She was quiet for a moment. "Hey, Lily . . . maybe we should talk to Randy about forming an alliance. Y'know, to keep the three of us around till the end."

"Not a bad idea," said Lily. "Let's do it when we get back."

To continue, turn to page 84.

"Technically," said Zoe, "Randy came in second. So I guess it's only fair that I choose him."

"Well, Randy, it's your lucky day," said Jake. "You two are going to be taken to an isolated spa we have at one end of the island where you can use the pool, the hot tub, and the gym. You'll have full access to a kitchen and game room. And, you'll get to sleep in real beds tonight."

"That rocks," said Randy. "Zoe, thank you so much!"

Zoe smiled. She couldn't help but think that she would have had more fun if she had chosen Lily.

"The remaining players will have to decide which camp to set up in," said Jake, "and then move all the stuff from the camp being left behind."

April, Carlos, and Lily decided that Pom Likit was a better camp since it had more shelter. As they made their way to Kwam Gla base to start moving stuff, the remainder of the newly formed team got to know one another better.

"Y'know," said Lily. "I kind of thought Zoe would pick me. I mean, we've been through a lot together."

"Just goes to show you that you can't be sure about anything anymore," said Carlos.

"Right," said April. "I had to vote off a really good friend last night."

"I know," said Lily. "But I've helped Zoe out a lot. I thought she'd return the favor."

Meanwhile, over on the other side of the island, Zoe

and Randy were swimming in the pool, batting an inflatable beach ball around.

"Zoe, this is awesome," Randy said. "But how come you didn't pick Lily? I mean, you guys are so tight."

"Randy," said Zoe. "We're playing a game. The best person wins. You performed really well in the last challenge, so I figured it was only fair to reward you for it. Hey, how do you feel about alliances?"

"What about 'em?" asked Randy.

"I think we should team up with Lily and make sure that the original Pom Likit team makes it to the final three," answered Zoe.

"Maybe," said Randy.

"What do you mean, 'maybe?'" asked Zoe. "I just gave you this huge reward and now you're saying 'maybe?'"

"Zoe," said Randy, "I told you I was grateful you brought me along. But that has nothing to do with playing the game. I've always been a little wary of alliances. Let's just see what happens."

Zoe nodded but frowned. She hadn't thought she would have to worry about anyone from Pom Likit voting against her.

To continue, turn to page 84.

"Welcome back," Jake greeted everyone two days later. "This will be your first Immunity Challenge as a combined tribe. As I've said before, only one of you will win Immunity from tonight's Tribal Council. And instead of the Immunity idol, one of you will get to wear this."

He held up a leather cord that had a smaller version of the idol attached to it.

"Ooh, that looks cool," said Zoe. "It'll look really good around my neck."

"Well, you have to earn it first," April said.

Zoe started to respond to April, then thought better of it. She shrugged her shoulders and turned back to Jake.

"Okay, let's get started," said Jake. "Think you've been paying attention to your surroundings? Today we're going to find out. In 'Local Lore,' you'll all be asked a bunch of questions, and you'll have to write down your answers. There will be questions about the local plants, animals, and more."

The five players sat down behind a table while Jake took a seat across from them. Each player had his or her own piece of paper and a pencil, and there were small dividers placed in between them so that no one could cheat.

"Question one," began Jake. "What is the name of the island we're on?"

"That's easy," said Carlos. "Who doesn't know that?"

"Ready?" asked Jake. "Question two. What is dengue fever?"

This time there was a noticeable pause as the players considered their answers. April and Lily were soon scribbling.

"Still think it's so easy, Carlos?" asked Zoe.

"Zoe," warned Jake. "No talking."

"Sorry," said Zoe.

"Next question," said Jake. "Name three edible plants found on the island. You can include plants that need to be boiled before eating."

Carlos threw down his pencil in frustration as the others feverishly wrote their answers. "I didn't think there would be any *tests,*" he whispered. "I mean, this isn't *school.*"

"Again," said Jake. "No talking. And Carlos, you're right, this isn't school. But these are things you should have known in order to get by here."

In the end April, with all her knowledge about wild edibles and wildlife, got almost a perfect score.

"April," said Jake. "Come on up here. You've won Immunity for this round. This means that no one can vote you off the island at the next Tribal Council. You're safe for at least a few more days."

The remaining players were still getting used to the merger. The former tribe members of Kwam Gla were sticking together, as were the former members of Pom Likit.

April and Carlos took a walk under the pretense of collecting wood.

"So," said Carlos, "you must be totally psyched that no one can vote for you."

"It's pretty cool," said April. "But I'm still not sure who to vote for."

"That's easy," said Carlos. "Zoe. She's so loud. And bossy."

"Maybe," said April. "Lily and Randy are strong competitors, though. Might be a good idea to get rid of one of them."

"I'm just nervous that the three of them will gang up on me," said Carlos.

"You never know what people are thinking," said April. "Maybe they've spent so much time together that they're sick of each other."

"That's what I'm hoping," said Carlos.

Meanwhile, the three former Pom Likit teammates were discussing the same thing back at camp.

"It's gotta be Carlos," said Zoe. "He's a little twerp. He doesn't deserve to win."

"Well, we don't have any ties to him," said Lily. "And since we can't vote for April, I'd tend to agree with you, Zoe."

"How about you?" Zoe asked Randy.

"Probably," said Randy.

"'Probably?'" asked Zoe. "What does *that* mean?"

"It means what it means," said Randy. "I'll probably vote for him."

Zoe looked at Lily as Randy walked away. "Do you think we're in trouble?"

"To be honest," said Lily, "I don't know what to think anymore."

"So, how are you guys feeling tonight?" asked Jake as the new team took their seats at Tribal Council.

"Nervous," said Carlos.

"Tired," said Lily.

"Are you ready to cast your votes?" asked Jake. Everyone nodded reluctantly.

If you want Zoe to be voted off the island, turn to page 88.
If you want Carlos to be voted off the island, turn to page 89.

The team took their turns voting, and then Jake took a moment to get the urn, which contained the votes.

"One for Zoe," he read before opening another slip of paper. "Two for Zoe," he said.

Zoe started looking nervous as Jake unwrapped another one. "One for Carlos," he read. "Two for Carlos," he added after opening the next slip. He then picked up the last piece of paper and read it to himself. Then he turned it around as he said, "And one more for Zoe."

Zoe stood up and made her way to Jake.

"Zoe, any last words?" asked Jake.

"Go get 'em, guys," said Zoe. She looked directly at Randy. "Even you."

To continue, turn to page 90.

After the five voted, Jake retrieved the urn and read the votes.

"Carlos," he said, unwrapping a piece of paper. He unfurled two more at the same time. "Two for Zoe."

Zoe looked a bit panicked but relaxed a little when the next slip of paper said "Carlos."

Jake took the final slip of paper out of the urn and unwrapped it. He turned it so the five competitors could read it.

"Carlos," Jake read aloud. He looked up. "Come on up, buddy."

Carlos looked disappointed, but he tried to play it cool as Jake snuffed out his torch. "I had fun," he said before he walked away, leaving only four players behind.

To continue, turn to page 100.

The next day the remaining players gathered at their meeting place. Jake announced that from this point forward, there would be a challenge every day.

"You guys remember the old game Simon Says, right?" he asked. "Today you'll be playing 'Survivor Says.' Same idea, but with a pretty big prize. I'll be calling out commands, each one starting with 'Survivor says.' If you don't hear that first, do *not* move. Got it?"

The players nodded and got into position.

If you want Lily to win the reward,
turn to page 91.
If you want April to win the reward,
turn to page 93.

"I can't remember the last time I played this," said Carlos.

"I know," said April. "It's harder than I remember."

Jake started out slowly, but gradually sped up the rate at which he gave instructions. Randy was out first, followed by April.

"Survivor says jump up and down," said Jake.

Carlos and Lily started jumping.

"Survivor Says stop jumping," said Jake. "Survivor says stand on one foot."

"Can't you go any faster?" complained Carlos. "This is too easy."

"Careful what you wish for," called Randy.

"Survivor says stand on your other foot," said Jake. "Survivor says touch your head. Survivor says rub your stomach. Now both at the same time."

"Ha!" said Carlos. "I can do that."

He realized his mistake a few seconds later when Lily still hadn't touched her head.

"Awwww," whined Carlos as he went to join April and Randy.

"Lily?" said Jake. "It's your call. Who do you want to take with you for your reward?"

"I have to stay true to my Pom Likit tribe," Lily said. "I choose Randy."

"Congratulations, Randy," said Jake. "You and Lily will be having a special Thai feast prepared just for you. You'll be transported there via helicopter, so you'll get a tour of the surrounding area, too."

"That rocks!" said Randy.

"Come on," said Jake. "The helicopter is waiting."

"But I need to go get some stuff," said Lily.

"Bags have already been packed for you," said Jake. "We've even had some new clothes sent from home, so you can feel completely refreshed. You're in the home-stretch now; you deserve some rest and relaxation."

April and Carlos watched, trying not to look upset.

"Come on, Carlos," said April. "I'll whip us up something good for dinner."

"Something besides hermit crab and coconut?" asked Carlos sarcastically.

Late that night Randy and Lily returned to camp, where April and Carlos were just drifting off to sleep.

"That food was so incredible," Randy said.

"I know," said Lily. "And how awesome was the helicopter ride?"

"Amazing," said Randy.

"We're trying to sleep in here," yelled Carlos from inside the cave.

"Jealous?" asked Randy.

Carlos stood up and went outside. "Actually . . . yeah. So shut up already." He turned around and went back to his mat.

Randy looked at Lily and they burst out laughing.

To continue, turn to page 95.

April had always been great at Simon Says. Watching her was amazing—she operated almost like a machine following orders. Jake called out the commands rapidly, not leaving much time in between.

"Survivor says lift your right leg," said Jake. "Survivor says put it down. Survivor says lift your left leg. Put it down."

Both Carlos and Randy put their left legs down, and both realized their mistake a second too late.

After another minute of play Lily was knocked out too, leaving April victorious.

"April," said Jake, "who do you choose to come with you for your reward?"

"No question," said April. "My man, Carlos."

Carlos ran up to April excitedly. "What did we win?"

"Well, *April* won a Thai feast, including a helicopter tour to get there," said Jake. "And you're lucky enough to get to join her." He looked at Lily and Randy. "You two going to be okay?"

"Oh, sure," said Randy. "We're having clams for dinner with a side of mango."

"For a change," said Lily sarcastically. "Seriously, congratulations, you guys. Have fun tonight."

"We will," said Carlos.

When April and Carlos got back to camp late that night, Randy and Lily were still awake.

"How was it?" asked Lily.

"It was awesome," said Carlos. "First we had these dumplings. I don't know what was in them, but they were really good. Then we got soup, and there was coconut in it, and even though we've already eaten so much coconut, I didn't care because it tasted so much better. And then—"

"Are you sure you guys really want to be hearing this?" asked April.

"Sure," said Lily. "We may as well enjoy it vicariously through you."

"How was the helicopter ride?" asked Randy.

"Also awesome," said Carlos. "I never rode in a helicopter before. You could see the entire island."

"It was pretty cool," said April. "But I'm beat. See you guys in the morning."

"'Night, April," said Carlos. "Thanks again." He turned back to Randy and Lily. "So, anyway . . ."

To continue, turn to page 95.

"Today's Immunity Challenge is to test how well you really know each other," said Jake. "But before we start playing, I'm going to need to take back the Immunity necklace. April?"

April walked up and handed it over a little reluctantly.

"Thanks," said Jake. "Now, back to the challenge. I would imagine that you've gotten to know your remaining team members fairly well. Plus, we're evenly matched, with two of you from the original Kwam Gla team and two of you from Pom Likit. So you should at least know a lot about one of your current teammates."

Carlos looked a little worried. Paying attention to details wasn't exactly his strong point.

Jake began by asking relatively simple questions, like what states the others were from. However, it soon became more difficult.

"Carlos, name April's luxury item."

Carlos looked frantically at April, hoping she could somehow send him the answer telepathically.

"Um . . . ," he stalled. "She brought . . . well, she likes making us all sorts of teas and stuff from berries. . . . Did she bring a cookbook?"

"No," Jake said. "She brought her stuffed manatee."

"Marina," said April. "She's a good luck charm, and so far she's been working pretty well."

"April," said Jake. "How many brothers and sisters, if any, does Lily have?"

"Two?" asked April.

"No," Jake answered. "Three. Randy, bonus point for you if you can tell me how many brothers and sisters Carlos has."

"I think it's two sisters and a brother," said Randy.

"You got it, " said Jake, turning to Lily. "Lily. Who is Randy's idol?"

Lily thought. She had no idea. Randy was good at sports—maybe an athlete? He was close with his family, so maybe one of his parents? Or a teacher?

"I'm not sure," Lily stammered. "Um . . . I'm going to go with his dad."

Randy and Jake both shook their heads.

"Randy's hero is David Blaine," said Jake.

"Remember?" Randy said. "All those magic tricks I like to practice?"

Lily slapped her forehead. "Duh . . ."

"Randy," said Jake. "Immunity is yours this time around, taking you one round closer to the grand prize." He placed the necklace on Randy, who touched it proudly.

"See you guys tonight," said Jake.

"Must feel pretty good to have Immunity, huh?" Lily said to Randy on their way back to the campsite.

"Yup," said Randy.

"So, I know you're not into alliances, but I can count on you, right?" said Lily.

"Yup," said Randy again. "Don't worry, Lily. I thought about it, and I'm taking you with me to round eight."

"Thanks," said Lily. "So have you decided whether

you are going to vote for April or Carlos?"

"Not sure yet," said Randy. "April is a really good competitor, so it would be smart to send her home. But she's also more fun to have around than Carlos, who's actually proving to be not so bad a competitor after all. So . . . I don't know."

"I have a lot to figure out before tonight," said Lily.

If you want Carlos to be voted off the island, turn to page 98.
If you want April to be voted off the island, turn to page 99.

The foursome voted and Jake retrieved the urn. He took out two at a time.

"Two for Carlos," he read. He then unwrapped another one. "One for April. And"—Jake picked up the last piece of paper and opened it—"the final vote is for Carlos."

"Aw, man," said Carlos, standing up.

"Sorry, buddy," Jake said, "but the tribe has spoken."

To continue, turn to page 110.

"Welcome back," said Jake. "How are you guys doing?"

"Okay," said Lily.

"It's getting down to the wire," said Jake.

"Yeah," said Carlos. "So let's get this over with."

The four remaining players cast their votes one at a time and then returned to their seats to wait for Jake to bring the urn over. Jake pulled out two pieces of paper. One was for Carlos, and one was for April. He then unwrapped one more. "April," he read, looking a little surprised.

Jake picked up the final slip of paper and opened it. "Well," he said, turning it around. "April."

April came up to Jake, tipping forward her torch. She looked a little disappointed, but covered it with a small smile.

"Great game," said Jake. "You played well."

"Thanks," April said. "And now I get to go chill out."

To continue, turn to page 128.

"How are you all holding up?" Jake asked the next morning.

"Fine," said Zoe.

"Ready to play," said Randy.

"Glad to hear it," said Jake. "Because from now on, there will be a challenge every day.

"Your next Reward Challenge," he continued, "is the Survivor Olympics. It includes throwing both a coconut 'discus' and a bamboo 'javelin,' seeing how far you can jump, and walking across a balance beam . . . in the water."

If you want Lily to win the reward,
turn to page 101.
If you want Randy to win the reward,
turn to page 103.

"Lily," said Zoe, "you're going to rock this, with all your gymnastics and dance experience."

"Yeah," said Lily. "But that doesn't help me with throwing a coconut!"

Randy started out strong with his performance in the coconut throw and bamboo spear throw, but then faltered on the balance beam. After only a few seconds on the beam, he slipped off and was disqualified.

The three remaining players were pretty evenly matched. But Lily was able to excel both in the jump and on the beam.

"Congrats, Lily," said Jake. "Looks like you're the winner of this Reward Challenge. Who are you going to choose?"

"I can only choose one?" said Lily.

"You know the rules," said Jake.

"Then I have to go with Zoe," said Lily.

Zoe grinned and joined Lily.

"You two are each going to get to talk to a member of your family," said Jake. "But this time, you'll be able to see them as well, using a videophone."

"That's awesome!" said Lily. "Thank you!"

"At least we'll get to see the real thing pretty soon, right?" Randy said to April.

"Since the longer we last here, the longer it'll be that we see 'em, I hope it's later rather than sooner," answered April.

Zoe and Lily were taken to a nearby hut where there was electronic equipment set up. Zoe wanted to talk to her dad, and Lily to her oldest sister, Nina. There were two screens set up, and Jake dialed the numbers.

"Dad," said Zoe, "it's so good to talk to you!"

"You too, kiddo," said Zoe's father, laughing. "So when ya coming home? We got some baseball to watch."

"I'll be there soon," said Zoe. "But first I gotta win this thing."

"Atta girl," he said.

Meanwhile Lily couldn't help but cry a bit when she saw her sister.

"Lily," said Nina, "don't cry. We'll see you soon."

"I know," said Lily. "I guess I didn't realize how much I missed you until I saw your face. . . ."

"How's it going?" asked Nina.

"Good," said Lily. "I'm doing well."

"Are you going to win two hundred thousand dollars and buy me a car?"

Lily laughed. "Send all your good karma my way, okay?"

After a few more minutes Jake told the girls they needed to wrap it up. They did, and then returned to camp to rest up for the next challenge feeling a little more homesick than before, but also a little happier.

To continue, turn to page 104.

Everyone did well with the coconut throw, but Zoe, April, and Lily all had trouble with the bamboo spear throw; they just couldn't get it to go very far. Randy, on the other hand, had been on his school's track-and-field team, so he was able to send it sailing. That alone almost gave him enough to win the challenge. Lily pulled closer with her agility on the balance beam, but ultimately, Randy's overall performance gave him the win.

"Randy," said Jake, "it's your choice who will join you."

"April," said Randy. "That way I don't have to choose one of my original teammates over another one."

"Cool," said April. "Thanks, Randy."

"Nice thinking, Randy," said Jake. "But actually, this time around, we have something for all of you. Your friends and families have recorded videotaped messages. Randy and April, you'll get to watch yours first, and we'll serve you dinner while you watch. Lily and Zoe, you'll get to watch yours later on, and since you didn't win, no dinner included."

"Who cares?!" said Zoe. "That's still awesome!"

Randy and April laughed at the messages their friends and relatives had recorded for them, while enjoying whatever food they wanted. April had eggplant parmigiana, while Randy had spare ribs.

"Do we have to go back?" April asked Jake.

"Yes," said Jake, "but you guys are doing great. Just hang in for a few more days."

"That's my plan," said Randy.

To continue, turn to page 104.

Jake approached the foursome on the beach bright and early the next morning.

"Randy?" he asked. "I think you have something for me?"

Randy got up and reluctantly handed the Immunity necklace to Jake, who held it high above his head. "This is up for grabs again," he said. "To determine who gets to wear it next, you'll be playing 'Hang On Tight.' Follow me."

Jake led the way into the jungle, eventually stopping at a large net that was set up underneath the canopy of trees.

"If you'll look up," Jake said as he pointed skyward, "you'll see some trapeze bars. There are four, one for each of you. You'll each need to stay suspended from your bar—using feet, hands, knees, whatever—for as long as you can. You just can't sit on the bar. The last one hanging wins Immunity. Not too hard, right?"

"Sure, if you don't look down," said Zoe.

"Come on, Zoe," said Randy. "You were great at rock climbing."

"I was *harnessed* while rock climbing!" said Zoe.

The four made their way up a ladder and settled themselves onto the bars. For the first half hour, no one complained—they just joked with one another and literally hung out. But then Zoe's leg started cramping badly.

"Hang on, Zoe," said Lily.

"Y'know what," said Zoe, "it's not worth it." She fell to the net, rubbing her leg.

Next to go was Randy, ten minutes later. By that point April was switching from leg to arm quite frequently. Lily hung from her knees calmly, eyes closed. April tried talking to her.

"Lily, what's your secret? Come on, how do you do it?"

But Lily wouldn't budge. She barely moved a muscle.

"She's in Zen mode," called Randy. "She's totally in the zone. April, you might as well give up."

But that only fueled April more. The two of them hung on for another forty minutes. Finally April couldn't ignore the trembling of her muscles any longer. She held on by her hands for a few more minutes and then finally succumbed, falling down into the net below.

A few seconds later Lily smiled and let herself fall to the net.

If you want Randy voted off the island next, turn to page 106.
If you want Zoe voted off the island next, turn to page 108.

Before they left camp for Tribal Council, April approached Zoe and Lily.

"I've been thinking," she said. "How cool would it be to have a final three of all girls?"

"Yeah," said Zoe. "But Randy's our friend."

"He's a great player and people like him," said April. "He'll be hard to beat."

"I think we're all pretty hard to beat at this point," said Lily.

April shrugged. "Look, I'm just trying to form an alliance, and I thought it would be nice if the girls stuck together. I think Randy's a threat to all of us. But you guys have to do what you think is best."

Randy soon joined them, and the four made their way to Tribal Council.

"Nice job today, Lily," said Jake as they all sat down. "Seemed like you could have stayed up there forever."

"Thanks," Lily said. She touched the Immunity necklace she wore around her neck.

"Well," said Jake. "It's that time again. Time to vote."

One by one, the players cast their votes. Jake went to retrieve the urn. This time he pulled all four slips out at once, unwrapping all of them and stacking them one on top of the other.

"Randy," he read. "April. And one more for Randy."

Randy made eye contact with April. He sensed that she had been the one who most wanted him to go; after all, they had been from different teams and had no real loyalty to each other.

Jake read from the final piece of paper. "Randy."

Zoe breathed a sigh of relief. She had made it into the final round. Randy picked up his torch and saluted the three remaining players.

"Happy trails, guys," he said. "Oops. I mean 'girls.'"

To continue, turn to page 135.

Zoe and Lily headed to Tribal Council together.

"It's great that you have Immunity," said Zoe. "Not that you would have been voted off anyway—everyone likes you."

"Everyone likes you, too," said Lily.

"I'm not sure," said Zoe. "I know I can be loud and dramatic and whatever, but I also think I've been a solid player and dependable. Right?"

"Definitely," said Lily.

"So why am I so scared?" asked Zoe.

Lily put her arm around her friend. 'Well, if it makes you feel any better, I'm not voting for you."

"You better not," said Zoe.

Meanwhile April and Randy trailed behind.

"Zoe's really tough," said April.

"That she is," said Randy.

"I'm voting her out," said April. "I think it would be smart for you to do the same."

"I'm not sure," said Randy.

"Randy, come on," said April. "Let's make a deal. I won't vote for you and you won't vote for me. Who knows who Lily and Zoe are voting for. You need me."

Randy thought about it. "You may be right. We'll see."

The four players approached the Tribal Council site and took their seats. Jake showed up a minute later.

"How are you all holding up?" he asked.

"Okay," said Lily.

"Of course you're okay," said April a little testily. "You have Immunity!"

"April," said Jake. "A little nervous?"

"Trying not to be," said April. "But not totally suc-ceeding."

"You've all played very well," said Jake. "So you can take some comfort in that. But now, it's unfortunately time to vote one of you off. You know the drill."

One by one the players cast their votes. Jake brought the urn over to rest on a podium in front of them.

"April," he read off the first slip. A moment later he read, "Randy."

Randy and April exchanged glances. Zoe started to breathe a little easier, and stopped wringing her Yankees cap in her hands. Except her reaction was a little bit pre-mature.

"Zoe," read Jake. He unwrapped the final piece of paper and paused for a few seconds, staring at it. Then he turned it around, so the team could see that it said ZOE.

"It's time for me to go?" she asked.

"I'm afraid so," said Jake. "Come on up."

"Kick butt for me, okay?" Zoe said to Lily as she handed her the cap. Lily took it and hugged her friend.

"Absolutely."

To continue, turn to page 110.

The next morning Jake was waiting for the three remaining players on the beach.

"Welcome," he said. "And congratulations on making it to the final three. Today you'll participate in the final Immunity Challenge. Whoever wins will then have to choose who to take to the final Tribal Council. . . . Choose wisely, because then the entire group will return to sit on the jury and vote for the ultimate Survivor.

"You guys have handled lots of obstacles during your time here," continued Jake. "This next challenge is the king of all obstacle courses. It's called the "Over-the-Top Obstacle Course." There are five stages to this course. First you'll need to scale that climbing wall over there and come down the other side. Then you'll have to chew a native delicacy and swallow it. Next you'll hit the ocean and swim out to retrieve a flag—we've got three waiting on a buoy out there. Then you'll swim back to shore and go back to the climbing wall, scaling the other side. Finally, after rappelling down, you'll run about two hundred meters toward a stake in the ground, waiting for you to throw your flag down over it. Got it?"

Three heads nodded.

"Good luck, then," said Jake.

If you want April to win Immunity,
turn to page 111.
If you want to Randy to win Immunity,
turn to page 121.

April, Lily, and Randy lined up, waiting for Jake to blow the whistle.

"On your mark," said Jake.

They tensed their muscles.

"Get set," continued Jake. "GO!"

The three remaining players took off running, headed for the climbing wall. They were evenly matched for the most part. They raced up and over the wall in record time and ran to the table. Before them were three bowls of something.

"What *is* this?" asked Lily, her nose wrinkled.

"Grubs," said Jake. "A good source of protein."

Lily looked back at the bowl of squirming "protein" and took a deep breath.

"Bon appetit," she said to her competitors.

The three players managed to chew and swallow the grubs, shuddering as they did, and then dove into the ocean, swimming evenly to the buoy. April pulled ahead as they swam back in, scrambling onto the sand before Randy and Lily. Lily unfortunately slipped in the sand, then Randy was able to pull ahead of April, reaching the stake a few seconds before her. April followed him, slamming her flag down over the stake.

"And we have a winner!" said Jake.

"April?" asked Randy. "But I came in first."

"Yes," said Jake. "But where's your flag?"

Randy looked around. He had forgotten about his flag and had dropped it on the sand. Normally even-tempered, this time Randy wasn't able to conceal his anger at himself for such a stupid mistake. He kicked some sand and stalked off, muttering to himself.

When he returned a few minutes later, Jake called April up to him. "You need to choose who's going to come to the final council with you tonight," he said.

[If you want April to choose Lily, turn to 113.
[If you want April to choose Randy, turn to 117.

April thought about it. Both Randy and Lily were well liked and good competitors. But Randy was really strong physically—something he had just proven—and the jury might reward him for that. Plus, she was more outgoing than Lily, which might work in her favor when pitted against her.

"I choose Lily," she said. "Sorry," she added, looking at Randy. He just shrugged. He was feeling defeated anyway.

To continue, turn to page 114.

That night the last two Survivors were escorted to their final challenge: facing the jury in their last Tribal Council. The jury would be composed of all their former teammates.

As the eight former players filed in, Jake said, "Welcome back and thank you for coming. We couldn't do this without you." He paused before remarking, "Wow, you guys look clean."

Everyone laughed for a minute, glad Jake had broken the tension a bit.

"We're here tonight to discover who will win the game," he continued. "Who has managed to outwit, outplay, and outlast nine very strong, worthy opponents. Only one of you will go home with the two hundred thousand dollars and the title of 'Sole Survivor.'"

He turned to the final two players. "You'll each have a chance to state why you think you should be the ultimate Survivor. And then one of your former teammates will have the opportunity to ask a question. Ready? Then let's begin.

"April, you're up first."

April nodded and stood up. She smiled.

"Hi, guys," she began. "I don't like giving long speeches, so this'll be brief. Basically, I've loved my time here. I came looking for an adventure, and to make some friends, and to play the game well but also fairly. I think I've achieved all of those things. I don't think anyone can argue that my energy ever flagged, or that you couldn't rely on me to give it my all. I would love to win the grand prize, and I hope you feel I deserve to. Thanks."

She sat down, and Lily stood up.

"When I arrived here a month ago," Lily said, "I wasn't sure how long I would last. I was a little nervous about making friends, about people being cutthroat, about being able to maintain my strength. But I was able to stay calm, and I was able to rely on both the friends I made and on myself. I quickly learned who I could and couldn't trust. I think that I remained calm in tense situations, and that I am worthy of the grand prize."

"Now let's see if the jury has any questions for you," Jake said. He called on Peter to ask a question.

"April and Lily," he began, "I'm not going to be typical and ask you to tell me why you should win. I want you to tell me why your opponent should lose."

April and Lily glanced a bit worriedly at each other. Trust Peter to come up with something devious like that.

"I have nothing really bad to say about Lily," said April. "She's been nothing but supportive and a good player. But I guess I don't really see her as a leader. She keeps to herself a lot, while I like to come in and take charge. I think that in a game like this, you have to be more powerful."

"Well," countered Lily, "April could be a bit too loud at times. It could be distracting. Not every word has to be shouted. Although maybe that was her strategy—to not just outplay everyone else, but to outyell them too."

"Thanks," said Peter. He smirked, glad that he was able to break April and Lily's concentration a bit.

"Okay," said Jake. "The eight of you will now vote. April and Lily will not vote, since we can assume they would cancel each other out. Remember, this time you're voting for the person you want to *win,* not who you want to be sent home."

A few minutes later Jake tallied the votes, reading them aloud one at a time

"April . . . Lily . . . Lily . . . April . . . April . . . Lily . . . April," he paused, looking at the two finalists.

"One more vote," said Jake. "There could be a winner or there could be a tie. . . . Are you ready?"

Both girls nodded. Jake opened the final slip of paper.

"APRIL!" said Jake. "You are our Sole Survivor! Congratulations!"

April started crying as everyone came down to engulf her in a hug. She smiled up at Jake as he presented her with an oversized, mocked-up check for $200,000.

"April," said Lily, "no hard feelings about what I said, right? I'm really excited for you."

"Hard feelings?" said April. "No way! This ROCKS!"

THE END

April knew that Lily didn't really have any enemies, so it would be dangerous to go up against her in the final round. Randy was also pretty well liked, but he had more of a temper than Lily, and that may have turned off some players along the way.

"I choose Randy," she said, avoiding eye contact with Lily. But Lily was fine—she hugged April and Randy good-bye and was escorted off to meet up with the rest of the jury.

To continue, turn to page 118.

That night the last two Survivors were escorted to their final challenge: facing the jury in their last Tribal Council. The jury would be composed of all their former teammates.

As the eight former players filed in, Jake said, "Welcome back and thank you for coming. We couldn't do this without you." He paused before remarking, "Wow, you guys look clean."

Everyone laughed for a minute, glad Jake had broken the tension a bit.

"We're here tonight to discover who will win the game," he continued. "Who has managed to outwit, outplay, and outlast nine very strong, worthy opponents. Only one of you will go home with the two hundred thousand dollars and the title of 'Sole Survivor.'"

He turned to the final two players. "You'll each have a chance to state why you think you should be the ultimate Survivor. And then one of your former teammates will have the opportunity to ask a question. Ready? Then let's begin."

"Randy?" said Jake. "Why don't you start?"

"Okay," said Randy as he stood before his former teammates. "Hey, guys. Good to see you all back. I had an unbelievable time hanging out with all of you. I never could have predicted the adventures I've had here, and the things I've learned. I mean, I ate grubs. Willingly! So, even if I don't go home as the ultimate winner, I honestly feel like I've already gained something invaluable. Don't get me wrong, I'd like to win, and I think I deserve to. But I just wanted to let you know that I'm also just happy to have met you. Thanks."

"April?" said Jake.

"Hi, guys," she began. "I don't like giving long speeches, so this'll be brief. Basically, I've loved my time here. I came looking for an adventure, and to make some friends, and to play the game well but also fairly. I think I've achieved all of those things. I don't think anyone can argue that my energy ever flagged, or that you couldn't rely on me to give it my all. I would love to win the grand prize, and I hope you feel I deserve to. Thanks."

"Hannah?" asked Jake. "Do you have a question for Randy and April?"

"I do," said Hannah, standing up. "I want to know from each of you: What do you feel you brought to the island that no one else did?"

"I think I brought a real sense of team spirit," said April. "A committed, energetic sense of spirit."

"She did have spirit," said Randy. "And I'm grateful. But I think I offered unconditional and rational support to everyone here. I was generally able to distance myself from any drama and just play the game. And I think that's the sign of a champion."

"Thanks," said Hannah.

"Okay," said Jake. "The eight of you will now vote. Randy and April will not vote, since we can assume they would cancel each other out. Remember, this time you're voting for the person you want to *win,* not who you want to be sent home."

A few minutes later Jake tallied the votes and began reading them out loud. "Randy . . . April . . . April . . .

Randy . . . Randy . . . April. . . ." Jake looked up. "So far, you two are even. Any thoughts?"

"Either way," said April, "I know I played my best, and I'm proud."

"Ditto," said Randy.

Jake nodded and held up the final two pieces of paper, both of which said RANDY.

"RANDY!" said Jake. "You did it, man!"

He presented Randy with the grand prize: an oversized version of a check for $200,000.

Randy beamed as everyone came to congratulate him. April was the first one to hug him.

"Good game," she said.

"Thanks," Randy said. "It means a lot coming from such a tough opponent."

"Well, if you want to share . . . ," said April.

Randy smiled. "Maybe next time around, dude."

THE END

Lily, Randy, and April took their spots at the starting line, tensely waiting for Jake to give them the go-ahead. At the sound of the whistle, they shot off, their sights on the climbing wall.

They started out neck and neck, with Randy taking a slight lead as they scaled the wall. When he jumped down and ran to the table with the "delicacy," he dug right in. But when April and Lily got there a moment later, they weren't so eager.

"What is this?" asked April.

"Grubs," said Jake.

"And what exactly are grubs?" said April. Lily, meanwhile, had started biting one and was chewing fast, her eyes shut. Randy was almost done.

"They're insect larvae," said Jake. "You can eat them boiled or raw. Better start, you're losing valuable time."

April, who had reluctantly suspended her vegetarianism for her stay on the island simply because she knew she needed to eat fish to stay healthy, had to draw the line at this. The grubs were still alive!

"I'm sorry," she said. "I can't do it."

"Then I'm afraid you'll have to be disqualified," said Jake.

Meanwhile both Lily and Randy had finished and were near the water. Randy dove in and swam out to the buoy. He snatched a flag and started back, passing Lily on the way. He arrived on shore and ran the remainder of the race as if his feet were on fire, slamming his flag down over the post before Lily could even run halfway there.

"Nice job, Randy," said Jake. "And congratulations on making it to the final two. Now you have the ultimate decision to make: who you'll choose to take with you to tonight's Tribal Council."

If you want Randy to choose April,
turn to page 123.
If you want Randy to choose Lily,
turn to page 124.

Randy pondered his choice carefully. Both Lily and April were popular. But Lily was generally calm and soft-spoken, while April was more outgoing and occasionally overly energetic. It was more likely that she had annoyed some people during the past month, and so she was a better person to go up against in the final Council.

"I choose April," he said. "May the best ma—um, *person*, win."

To continue, turn to page 118.

It was a tough decision. Randy liked both Lily and April, and thought they had each done a good job over-all. But April had more spunk—she had lifted people's spirits often. The jury might remember that and want her to win. Plus, Lily was one of Randy's original Pom Likit teammates; he felt he owed her this one last shot at the grand prize.

"I choose Lily," he said.

To continue, turn to page 125.

That night the last two Survivors were escorted to their final challenge: facing the jury in their last Tribal Council. The jury would be composed of all of their former teammates.

As the eight former players filed in, Jake said, "Welcome back and thank you for coming. We couldn't do this without you." He paused before remarking, "Wow, you guys look clean."

Everyone laughed for a minute, glad Jake had broken the tension a bit.

"We're here tonight to discover who will win the game," he continued. "Who has managed to outwit, outplay, and outlast nine very strong, worthy opponents. Only one of you will go home with the two hundred thousand dollars and the title of 'Sole Survivor.'"

He turned to the final two players. "You'll each have a chance to state why you think you should be the ultimate Survivor. And then one of your former teammates will have the opportunity to ask a question. Ready? Then let's begin.

"Randy?" said Jake. "Why don't you start?"

"Okay," said Randy as he stood before his former teammates. "Hey, guys. Good to see you all back. I had an unbelievable time hanging out with all of you. I never could have predicted the adventures I've had here, and the things I've learned. I mean, I ate grubs. Willingly! So, even if I don't go home as the ultimate winner, I honestly feel like I've already gained something invaluable. Don't get me wrong, I'd like to win, and I think I deserve to. But I just wanted to let you know that I'm also just happy to have met all of you. Thanks."

Randy sat down. Lily rubbed the palms of her hands on her legs before standing up. She cleared her throat.

"When I arrived here a month ago," she said, "I wasn't sure how long I would last. I was a little nervous about making friends, about people being cutthroat, about being able to maintain my strength. But I was able to stay calm, and I was able to rely on both the friends I made and on myself. I quickly learned who I could and couldn't trust. I think that I remained calm in tense situations, and that I am worthy of the grand prize."

"Brenna," said Jake. "You have the floor."

"Hi," said Brenna. "I just want to start out by saying that I think it's great that you lasted this long and did so well. I felt badly about wanting to leave so soon after I got here. And to tell you the truth, I felt a little 'homesick' for you guys after I left.

"I think I know why you each think you should win. But I'd like for you to tell me why you think your opponent should win."

"Hmm," said Lily. "Well, Randy's been a friendly, no-nonsense guy from the beginning. He rarely complained, and he never slacked off."

"And Lily," said Randy, "could stay calm in the middle of a monsoon. Luckily we didn't have to find out if that's actually true, but I'm telling you, she is incredibly peaceful, and it provided a nice model for the rest of us."

"Thanks," said Brenna. "And good luck to both of you."

"Okay," said Jake. "The eight of you will now vote. Randy and Lily will not vote, since we can assume they would cancel each other out. Remember, this time you're voting for the person you want to *win*, not who you want to be sent home."

A few minutes later Jake tallied the votes, reading them slowly aloud.

"Randy," he began. "And one for Lily. Another for Lily. And yet another for Lily."

Jake looked up at Randy. "How are you doing?"

"Fine," said Randy. "Let's hear the rest."

"Okay," said Jake. "One for Randy." He unwrapped the final two votes and held them up. Both said "Lily."

"Lily," said Jake. "You're our new Sole Survivor!"

Lily couldn't stay calm any longer. She cheered at the top of her lungs as the group crowded around her. Randy even put her up on his shoulders.

"How does it feel?" shouted Zoe up to Lily.

"It feels . . . amazing," cried Lily.

THE END

"So," continued Jake, "today you're going to be doing some construction work. The name of this challenge is 'Build Your Way to Immunity.' Carlos, you may be at a slight advantage here, since you had to help construct your own shelter with Kwam Gla. But then again, you weren't doing that all by yourself.

"We have three building stations set up, one for each of you. You won't be able to see one another during the competition. We've provided each one of you with enough raw materials to build a small hut. You'll be on the clock. The first person to finish his or her hut—and it has to be sturdy—wins the challenge. Keep in mind that you can be creative with this, but there are some materials that just won't fit together. You'll need to figure out which way is best."

The three were shown to their stations, where they inspected the materials they'd been given. Bamboo. Tree branches. Palm fronds. Sticks. A little bit of twine, which was a gift.

"Everyone at your stations?" asked Jake. "Everyone had time to check out what you'll be working with?"

Carlos, Lily, and Randy all nodded to both questions.

"Then good luck," Jake said as he blew the whistle to start the race.

It quickly became clear that the three had very different approaches. Carlos jumped right in, slapping materials together eagerly and then trying again when they didn't hold together. Randy took a minute to inspect what he had and then started building, but soon became frustrated when he couldn't get the materials to stick together.

Lily, on the other hand, silently surveyed the materials for a while—much longer than either Carlos or Randy had. She then calmly began stacking branches together, tying them with twine, and using the palm fronds for overhead shelter.

An hour later, Lily was the only one who had a genuine shelter ready.

"We have a winner," said Jake. "Lily, you've got a ticket to the final Tribal Council. Who will you choose to go with you?"

If you want Lily to choose Randy,
turn to page 130.
If you want Lily to choose Carlos,
turn to page 131.

Lily pondered her decision calmly, just like she did almost everything. Carlos was a bit immature. She wasn't sure she wanted to provide him with any opportunity to win the grand prize; she didn't think he deserved it. Plus, she felt some allegiance to Randy, whom she'd known since the beginning.

"I choose Randy," she said.

To continue, turn to page 125.

Lily surveyed the two guys in front of her. She liked Randy a lot, but he had more of a chance of beating her in the final Council. He hadn't been anything but a strong player and an easygoing teammate for the most part. Carlos, on the other hand, had annoyed his share of players. Lily knew if she chose Carlos, she would more than likely end up the winner.

"Carlos," Lily said. "You're coming with me."

To continue, turn to page 132.

That night the last two Survivors were escorted to their final challenge: facing the jury in their last Tribal Council. The jury would be composed of all their former teammates.

As the eight former players filed in, Jake said, "Welcome back and thank you for coming. We couldn't do this without you." He paused before remarking, "Wow, you guys look clean."

Everyone laughed for a minute, glad Jake had broken the tension a bit.

"We're here tonight to discover who will win the game," he continued. "Who has managed to outwit, outplay, and outlast nine very strong, worthy opponents. Only one of you will go home with the two hundred thousand dollars and the title of 'Sole Survivor.'"

He turned to the final two players. "You'll each have a chance to state why you think you should be the ultimate Survivor. And then one of your former teammates will have the opportunity to ask a question. Ready? Then let's begin.

"Carlos?" said Jake. "Why don't you start?"

Carlos stood up almost shyly. "Hi. I know a lot of you think of me as young. And I guess I am. But I think that I've grown up a lot by being here. I learned a lot from all of you. I still can't really believe that I've lived here for the past month and done some of the things I did. I can't wait to tell my friends and family all the stories I now have. And I'm going to miss all of you."

"Lily?" said Jake. "You're up."

"When I arrived here a month ago," Lily said, "I

wasn't sure how long I would last. I was a little nervous about making friends, about people being cutthroat, about being able to maintain my strength. But I was able to stay calm, and I was able to rely on both the friends I made and on myself. I quickly learned who I could and couldn't trust. I think that I remained calm in tense situations, and that I am worthy of the grand prize."

"Zoe?" asked Jake. "Do you have a question for Lily and Carlos?

"Yup," said Zoe. "It's pretty basic. Why should we vote for you?"

"I've been committed to supporting my team," said Lily, "while playing the game well. I never cheated or gossiped. I tried to stay calm, cool, and collected at all times. I helped gather food, and kept up a clean campsite. And I competed really well, which is why I'm still here."

"Lily was a good player," said Carlos. "Better than me, even. But I think if there was a 'Most Improved Player' award, I would get it. I've changed and grown more than anyone here. I bet none of you would have predicted that the loud little kid from Texas would place in the final two. And yet, here I am. Thanks, guys, for giving me a shot."

"Okay," said Jake. "The eight of you will now vote. Lily and Carlos will not vote, since we can assume they would cancel each other out. Remember, this time you're voting for the person you want to *win,* not who you want to be sent home."

A few minutes later Jake tallied the votes and began to read them out loud.

"One for Lily," he said. "Another for Lily. One for Carlos. Another for Carlos. Yet another for Carlos."

Jake looked at Lily and Carlos.

"Lily," he asked, "are you nervous?"

Lily shook her head. "Nope."

"She doesn't get nervous!" said Carlos. "But I do!"

Jake chuckled and continued reading the votes. "Carlos. Carlos. And Carlos!

"Look at that, the comeback kid," said Jake. "Carlos, get up here!"

Jake handed Carlos his prize check for $200,000.

"Nice job," said Jake. "And you're right, you are definitely our Most Improved."

Everyone rushed Carlos, who was overcome with excitement.

"I can't believe it! Thanks, guys!" he said. "You're all invited to come horseback riding with me in Texas. 'Cause when I get home, I'm buying a horse!"

THE END

"Your last challenge," Jake continued, "is called 'Survivor of the Fittest.' It has a few elements. At the core, it's a mile-long race. But at every quarter-mile mark, you'll have a different task. At mark one, you'll be faced with a tile puzzle. The tiles will be out of order, and you'll have to arrange them to make a complete picture. At mark two, you'll need to use your wits to get some milk out of a coconut—something all of you should know how to do by now. At mark three, you'll need to jump rope for one hundred counts. But you can't get tripped up. If you miss a skip then the count starts over again. Any questions?"

Three sets of eyes watched his steadily.

"Then come on over here to the starting line," said Jake.

The girls stretched a bit, surveying the path they were to run. It cut through the rain forest, so at least the sun wouldn't be beating down on them.

"On your mark . . . get set . . . GO!" said Jake.

The three ran at a similar pace to the quarter-mile mark, where they were faced with three tables, each holding a set of mixed-up tiles. Lily was the first to figure out the picture was of an elephant, but she had two pieces reversed. Zoe finished the puzzle first, followed by April and finally Lily.

By the time Lily got to the half-mile mark, both April and Zoe had smashed their coconuts to produce a cupful of milk. Lily pounded her coconut against a rock and got the milk. She then ran to catch up with the others.

Both Zoe and April were solid rope jumpers, and

they were doing fine until Lily got there. A bit thrown by her arrival, April missed a beat and got tangled in her rope. She was furious at herself, but took a deep breath and started over.

Zoe hit a hundred a moment later and tossed her rope down, quickly getting back on the path toward the finish line. When she crossed it a few minutes later, she was so excited she was ready to burst.

"Awesome job," said Jake. "Now it's your call. Who are you going to take with you to the very last Tribal Council? April or Lily?"

If you want Zoe to choose April, turn to page 137.
If you want Zoe to choose Lily, turn to page 141.

This was a tough decision for Zoe. She liked both of the girls sitting in front of her. But she knew that she was more likely to get votes when compared to April. Lily's calmness and grace were too jarring a direct opposite of Zoe's brashness. Next to April, at least, Zoe knew she wouldn't come across as quite so loud.

"April," said Zoe. "It's your lucky day. You're coming with me."

To continue, turn to page 138.

That night the last two Survivors were escorted to their final challenge: facing the jury in their last Tribal Council. The jury would be composed of all their former teammates.

As the eight former players filed in, Jake said, "Welcome back and thank you for coming. We couldn't do this without you." He paused before remarking, "Wow, you guys look clean."

Everyone laughed for a minute, glad Jake had broken the tension a bit.

"We're here tonight to discover who will win the game," he continued. "Who has managed to outwit, outplay, and outlast nine very strong, worthy opponents. Only one of you will go home with the two hundred thousand dollars and the title of 'Sole Survivor.'"

He turned to the final two players. "You'll each have a chance to state why you think you should be the ultimate Survivor. And then one of your former teammates will have the opportunity to ask a question. Ready? Then let's begin.

"April?" said Jake. "Why don't you start?"

"Hi, guys," she began. "I don't like giving long speeches, so this'll be brief. Basically, I've loved my time here. I came looking for an adventure, to make some friends, and to play the game well but also fairly. I think I've achieved all of those things. I don't think anyone can argue that my energy ever flagged, or that you couldn't rely on me to give it my all. I would love to win the grand prize, and I hope you feel I deserve to. Thanks."

"So," said Zoe, "I'm still here. I can't believe it. A girl

from New York City, terrified of snakes, somehow made it in the rain forest. Who knew? I've really enjoyed spending time here, completely out of my 'natural habitat.' I know some of you probably think I'm loud, but please also consider how that motivated you at times. I'm really happy to have had this experience. I'll never forget it."

"Will?" asked Jake. "Do you have a question for Zoe and April?"

"Yes," said Will. "I think both of you are amazing. I'm really shy, so I admire Zoe for being so outgoing. And April, you were the first person to make an effort to be nice and include me. So, thank you for that.

"My question is: If you had the chance to do this all over again, would you?"

"Totally," said April. "No question. It was tough, and I stretched myself every day. But I learned so much about a different environment, and also that I could survive in a place that is so different from what I'm used to. I've met people from across the United States, people I never would have met otherwise. I wouldn't give up this experience for anything."

"I have to agree with April," said Zoe. "I can't believe how far I've come since the beginning. Being here has taught me that I can rely on myself. It's really been an amazing experience, and I'm only thirteen."

Will smiled at the two finalists. "Thanks."

"Okay," said Jake. "The eight of you will now vote. Zoe and April will not vote, since we can assume they would cancel each other out. Remember, this time you're voting for the person you want to *win*, not who you want to be sent home. Is everybody clear?"

A few minutes later Jake tallied the votes. Zoe. April. April. April. Zoe. Zoe. April. April.

"April," said Jake. "Nice work! Can you believe you've won two hundred thousand dollars?"

"No way," said April. She had tears in her eyes.

Zoe hugged April. "Congratulations . . . and if you ever want to spend some of that on a trip to New York, I'll be waiting!"

April was in shock. She was the Sole Survivor. She smiled at the group.

"You guys rock," she said. "And, I know it's corny, but you're all Survivors to me."

"So do we all get some of that cash?" asked Carlos.

"Nope," said April, smiling. "That's all mine!"

THE END

Zoe thought about it. April was a strong, confident personality. It seemed like she typically got what she wanted. Zoe wasn't sure she wanted to be pitted against someone like that when the final decisions were being made. Who knew what types of questions they'd have to answer. Zoe decided to stick with her original Pom Likit teammate instead.

"I choose Lily," said Zoe.

To continue, turn to page 142.

That night, the last two Survivors were escorted to their final challenge: facing the jury in their last Tribal Council. The jury would be composed of all their former teammates.

As the eight former players filed in, Jake said, "Welcome back and thank you for coming. We couldn't do this without you." He paused before remarking, "Wow, you guys look clean."

Everyone laughed for a minute, glad Jake had broken the tension a bit.

"We're here tonight to discover who will win the game," he continued. "Who has managed to outwit, outplay, and outlast nine very strong, worthy opponents. Only one of you will go home with the two hundred thousand dollars and the title of 'Sole Survivor.'"

He turned to the final two players. "You'll each have a chance to state why you think you should be the ultimate Survivor. And then one of your former teammates will have the opportunity to ask a question. Ready? Then let's begin.

"Zoe," said Jake. "Why don't you start?"

"So," said Zoe, "I'm still here. I can't believe it. A girl from New York City, terrified of snakes, somehow made it in the rain forest. Who knew? I've really enjoyed spending time here, completely out of my 'natural habitat.' I know some of you probably think I'm loud, but please also consider how that motivated you at times. I'm really happy to have had this experience. I'll never forget it."

She sat down and Lily took her place, standing and facing the jury of eight.

"When I arrived here a month ago," Lily said, "I wasn't sure how long I would last. I was a little nervous about making friends, about people being cutthroat, about being able to maintain my strength. But I was able to stay calm, and I was able to rely on both the friends I made and on myself. I quickly learned who I could and couldn't trust. I think that I remained calm in tense situations, and that I am worthy of the grand prize."

"Samuel?" asked Jake. "Do you have a question for Zoe and Lily?"

"Sure do," said Samuel. "Say you're each running for office. Tell me your top priority for your staff."

"Hmm," said Zoe. "Well, I would want everyone to feel represented, so I would hold weekly meetings to make sure that they all got a chance to voice their opinions."

"I would want there to be low stress levels," said Lily. "More gets done when people are calm and happy. So I would want to make sure people were taking time for themselves, doing what made them feel fulfilled."

"Interesting," said Samuel. "May the best candidate win."

"Okay," said Jake. "The eight of you will now vote. Zoe and Lily will not vote, since we can assume they would cancel each other out. Remember, this time you're voting for the person you want to *win*, not who you want to be sent home."

A few minutes later Jake tallied the votes and began to read them.

"Lily," he said. "Zoe. Another for Lily. And two more

for Zoe. That's two votes for Lily, and three votes for Zoe.

"How are you feeling?" Jake asked Lily and Zoe.

"Either way," said Lily, "I'll be satisfied."

"Me too," said Zoe. "But I think I'd be slightly more satisfied if the remaining votes were for me." She looked at Lily. "No offense."

"None taken," said Lily, smiling.

Jake returned to reading the votes aloud. "Zoe. Zoe. And . . . Zoe! The girl from New York is going home a winner! Zoe, come and get your prize!"

Zoe ran up to Jake and hugged him, accepting the huge mocked-up check he handed her. "You're all invited to New York!" she yelled to her former teammates. "All expenses on me!" Then she paused as everyone gathered around her.

"I'm serious," she said. "All of you *better* come to visit. We can even eat mango and go rock climbing, for old time's sake. But the best thing of all about where I'm from? The only snakes you'll find in New York City are the ones in the zoo."

THE END